Lance Armstrong's Crucifiers Get Dropped

&

Other Cycling and non-Cycling Stories

MITCHELL BELACONE

CONTENTS

LANCE ARMSTRONG'S CRUCIFIERS GET DROPPED

A couple of questions for those who condemn Lance Armstrong: have you ever been an integral part of raising close to half a billion dollars to aid people suffering from cancer? Did you get off your deathbed and win arguably the hardest sporting event in the world seven times consecutively? I ask because those are the two biggest differences between him and us. You should have chosen another whipping boy.

Take a gifted athlete in his early twenties who is made to realize the hard way that the only method to have a chance of winning in his chosen field was to do what almost all of the successful players were doing. Those were the unwritten rules of the game. The weaponry was often introduced and distributed by the older, wiser managers and medical professionals of their teams. Once on that path, there was no turning back without blighting or destroying your career.

Especially true for Lance, who had much to lose, starting with his wildly successful Cancer charity where he parked

$6,500,000 of his own money.

"Oh, but that doesn't make him right."

Ok, but certainly not nearly as wrong as the backseat crucifiers claim.

"But all his good was built on a lie."

The United States was built on broken promises, murdering almost an entire race of people in the process. Practically all that's left from that genocide are ironic jokes at Thanksgiving. More than two and a half million cancer survivors had been helped by Lance's charity as of 2012 when he stepped down. Take a moment to compare those truths.

"But he was mean to people, he destroyed lives."

Can you show me in the Union Cycliste Internationale (UCI) rule book where it states that attaining a charm school diploma will reduce your penalty? He was protecting himself, his foundation and the many others who played the same game by the "real world" rules they were given. When the jig was up, we were sold a simplistic good versus evil storyline and then led to take bloodthirsty satisfaction in bringing the hero down.

"He almost destroyed the sport."

The year before Lance started winning his Tours, the sport was in shambles thanks to the Festina affair. The whole Festina team was kicked out of the Tour de France for getting caught with drugs. People were arrested, other teams quit. During the race, the peloton twice got off their bikes and stopped the race in protest. Lance's Cinderella story and subsequent victories resuscitated the sport and the Tour.

... Indulge me, for a few pages before I get to the principals.

When a corporation moves a factory overseas to raise its stock price a few cents - putting thousands out of work, terrorizing families and burdening others in the middle class to subsidize our peers - after one news story, that's not a big deal for the press. Their corporate handlers are OK with it, because that's what they are: a corporation of the conglomerate, by the conglomerate, for the conglomerate, that shall not perish from the earth. Adios to us, but not to them.

The free press: free to answer to their corporate and political puppeteers. Donald Trump in large part owes his 2016 election win to the liberal press. He was the spectacle that sold advertising. Thus, they kept his name front and center. They helped elect him knowingly. On a personal basis, they might not have liked the result, but they had a bottom line to answer to. We understand, just do us all a favor and don't spend years preaching morality about a young man that went off course in a far less harmful game.

If you work on Wall Street: kindly consider stifling your thoughts on Lance. You're often trained to sell what's best for your company, which is not necessarily what's best for your client. You and your superiors survive by commissions, we get it. Every so often you get so greedy and deceitful you go bust, and the middle class is forced by your government to pay your bills and return you to your million-dollar salaries. Never mind the old ladies you took down with you that don't get bailed out.

As to the Lawyers: nearing my seventh decade, I can only speak from personal experience. If I paid one that had my best interests at heart, I felt lucky to the extreme. In my sample group were a half dozen that worked for the highest bidder. I can't go into more detail because it might force me to pay another law-bender to defend me, who in turn would likely betray me. So, to my small advocate circle, plead the Fifth on Lance, or may Shakespeare have his way with you. Henry VI: "The first thing we do, let's kill all the lawyers."

In Europe I recently paid a leading surgeon $20,000 for a procedure. Included were three days in the hospital, ten days with a physical therapist and a nurse who brought all the drugs I needed to my hotel room. My friend just had the same surgery in the U.S.A. as an outpatient, everything à la carte. The doctor and the hospital billed his insurance company $218,000. From my experience, surgeons sell what they do and knock what they don't do. Doctors often drag the elderly back for more office visits than needed to collect more insurance. Fine, you're a business, but don't try to pass yourself off as more than that. And to those doctors described in this mass-bankrupting-happy gang of thieves, please don't share your diagnosis on how heartless and dishonest Lance Armstrong was. … Yeah, Yeah, I know, but I'd have to hookup a truck battery to my laptop to have enough juice to give my opinion on health insurance companies.

If you are a politician in either US political party - I've learned to accept this truth - reality and the law are not part of your equation. Your existence and minions are little more than an exercise in rooting for the home team. You consistently put young men and women in harm's way for the profit of a few. You are there to serve the special interests that put you there. I would advise shutting up, but that would be bad advice, because it would leave you with next to nothing else to do. We don't need your referendum on Lance.

Hollywood has made numerous documentaries and films damning Armstrong. It doesn't take a PHD in deductive reasoning, or even a Boy Scout merit badge in that skill, to figure out that no single entity has done more to promote gun violence than our heroes in the television and motion picture industry. "It's only a movie" is your dodge until the

4

coin is flipped and you make a picture you proclaim "important, socially relevant", then you strut and pose like you're saving the world. I'd rather watch your brothers in arms, tobacco industry executives, yap on talk shows. Your collective douchebaggery, trying to act cute and silly while pimping yourselves, has run its course. For accuracy's sake, rename the Oscars, "The Merchants of Death Awards".

Of all the upside-down things in this world; these hollow-headed simpletons are the leading proponents and judge and jury of postpone culture. I believed that when Hollywood was making anti-McCarthyism movies (20 years after the fact), that if a guy like McCarthy ever showed up again, they would cave-in and rat even faster. I never could have dreamt they would be the new McCarthy. If hindsight is a radial keratotomy, I should have.

Thanks to founder Tarana Burke, it's certain the "Me Too" Movement has had an overall positive effect. Sadly, as a foul bi-product, Hollywood hijacked it and helped turn a portion of it into a mass media propagated home for kill-joys who weaponize liars of the attention-needy and money-grubbing variety. Bye-bye to "innocent until proven guilty". Those character assassins are labeled brave and heroes. When they take down an innocent, normally they get a pass. And they put a black hat on Armstrong? Pardon the religiously slanted editorial, but God help us all.

Our high-tech hero billionaires: find me a coffee shop without some internet surfer pecking away at the keyboard, proudly shining their backlit, fruit logo in your eyes. That cult was founded by a trendily dressed hipster who grudgingly gave the mother of his daughter the money to feed her. Lance Armstrong brought half a billion dollars to Cancer victims. Steven Jobs bullied everyone from underlings to waiters to Whole Foods employees. Ask Dr. Joseph Wiesel, who holds a patent for a device that detects an irregular heartbeat, what he thinks of today's Apple watch that detects irregular heartbeats. Or follow the court case.

Bill Gates, hero philanthropist. Microsoft has paid billions towards the multitude of lawsuits against it. In the words of the playwright Eugene O'Neill in *The Hairy Ape*: "For de small stealing dey puts you in jail, soon or late. But for de big stealing dey puts yo' picture in de paper an yo' statue in the Hall of Fame when you croaks." The above gangs make Armstrong look like a saint.

In the NFL, the Dallas Cowboys are no longer "America's Team", self-proclaimed or otherwise. The reason: most Americans bought and paid for the Denver Broncos on or around April 15th, 2022, making *them* "America's Team". Rob Walton of Walmart fame and his group bought the franchise for a record 4.65 billion dollars. Many Walmart workers are not paid a living wage, American taxpayers are obliged to pay approximately 6.2 billion dollars per year in the form of welfare, food stamps, etc., to compensate their employees. To be clear, this has nothing to do with their profit from the 70-80% of Chinese inventory they hawk. Americans covered those subsidies directly out of our taxes. They really put the "free" in their free enterprise. Bucking Broncos often suffer injuries at Rodeos. The woke thing to do is rename the team. How's about the Denver Sap-Makers? For the logo on the side of the helmet, put an extended arm holding a tin cup. Most media idol worships these fat-cat skinflints and their ilk, which makes sense when you consider that's who owns them. Leave those billionaires alone and deflect all that is evil on to the softer target; a kid who took the same drugs, but just rode his bike faster than the others. Mr. Walton of one of the richest families in the world, what can you buy us next with our left over 1.55 billion handout to you? Or keep the change and leave our perennially punked populous as it is.

At the time Lance Armstrong stepped down from The Lance Armstrong Foundation, the American Institute of Philanthropy Charity Watch gave the Foundation an A-, a higher rating than any other sports figure's charity. How did they rate your charity? How did they rate my charity?

The whistleblower Floyd Landis, who made more than a million dollars for ratting out Lance, had his Tour de France victory taken away for the same reason as Lance. If Floyd could collect the seeds from that irony and convert them to ones of cannabis, his marijuana farm would make him richer than Pablo Escobar ever was.

Then there's Tyler Hamilton, the goody two cleats who, when under the gun, used his dog's death as a pity play, which explains why he should have raced a bike without a top tube. His and many of his accused teammates' honesty was forced, not volunteered. They could have stepped away the first time their morality was affronted, as opposed to when the threat of jail stared them in the face. If they haven't yet, they should apologize to Lance, and then go away.

Emma O'Reilly was Lance's masseuse who also served as a drug mule. After she spilled the beans to journalist David Walsh, there's no doubting that Lance put her through hell. The big question: if she left the team over issues with Lance's coach, Johan Bruyneel, and, as she described, had a great relationship with Lance and called him a buddy, why snitch? Was it to get back at Bruyneel and to hell with Lance, leaving him as collateral damage? In an interview on Ireland's Public Service Media, on the subject of her own culpability, she stated, "I did very, very little." I'm not sure everybody else would describe getting rid of syringes, and picking up and delivering drugs as "very, very little". Lance ratted on nobody.

Speaking of Johan Bruyneel, other than win more, what did he do that was so different from other team directors of that era to receive a lifetime ban from the UCI? I can think of only one thing: he coached the most successful and famous bike racer who did what almost all the other riders did. The UCI used to protect Armstrong and others from their misdeeds; they were at the minimum enablers. They also believed they were helping the sport by doing so. That was until up until they jumped like rats from Armstrong's sinking ship and then attacked him and Bruyneel when they reached shore.

Greg LeMond lost his bike brand and claimed all kinds of horrors as a result of trying to expose Armstrong. Which, on its hands and knees, begs the question: if they were friends as both stated, why of all people did LeMond take it upon himself to try to annihilate his friend and damage Trek in the process? Trek was the manufacturer of Lance's bicycles as well as his own. Was he travelling the moral path and sticking up for the sport, or trying to reclaim his old throne as being the greatest American cyclist and sell more of his bikes to boot?

I followed and idolized LeMond since the day I sat in wool cycling shorts outside a bike shop and read about him in Velo News at the beginning of his career, when he beat a tough field, including a Russian Gold medalist, to win the 1981 Coors Classic. That reverence lasted until I heard him yapping about how it was impossible for Lance to be that good because he, LeMond, had a higher V02 max than Lance. The only thing that proved, scientifically and otherwise, was that Greg LeMond was not a great friend to have. What was he expecting from Lance in return anyhow? I'm guessing he saw the Tour de France stage where Armstrong was trying to gift the race to his breakaway companion and teammate. Lance told his friend: "Ride like you stole something." Two Germans came from behind and rode his teammate down. The pair presented no danger to Armstrong in the overall standings. Out of anger and revenge he risked his Tour by chasing them down through the curvy narrow streets of the finishing town to win the stage. Hey Greg: you fucked with that Texas Bull, and you got his horns.

A few questions for his wife Kathy LeMond. In the documentary *Slaying the Badger*, you claim that Lance's mom asked you, "How do I stop my son from being an asshole?" If that exchange really happened, do you think it possible Lance relayed a slight or an insult to his mom that he had offended you and Greg with, and she was humbling herself as compensation? Regardless of her motivation, the more important question is this: if Lance's mom didn't ride on the team bus, why did you throw her under it? Consider having your steerer tube checked.

Betsy Andrue, Lance's teammate's wife. You made it clear that you and your family were greatly damaged by Lance. For what it's worth, Lance admitted that and apologized for it. You won't fully accept it, partly because he won't fess up publicly to what you witnessed him telling his doctor from his hospital bed. Did you consider that maybe he had noble reasons as to why he didn't reveal that publicly? Is it possible that he was protecting others who witnessed that too? Maybe he was willing to come clean, but not so far as to put others at legal risk. Maybe your tattletale tour, full of sound and fury, signifying what can befall people who try to make moral decisions for others, never would have happened, if you let those folks carve their own path. Did it cross your mind that when Lance was in vehement denial mode, that he was also trying to shield the millions of cancer patients who took inspiration from his achievements? Your desire to see Frankie, and the race, become clean, was honorable. But did you expect the whole Armstrong winning train and the entire cycling culture to change just for your husband Frankie, without repercussions? Lance didn't design the model for cycling teams at that time, he just ran a tight ship within the given framework. You claimed that your husband "didn't take EPO for himself, because as a domestique (worker bee), he was never going to win the race." "It was for Lance." Of all the convoluted cop-outs. Does that mean he wasn't paid handsomely to train and race? Are you saying that he only rode his bike for the love of Lance? In a public forum that reached my television, you proclaimed, after a certain point, that if your husband were to take performance enhancing drugs, you would have divorced him. If you were my wife, and threatened me like that to the world, I would inject an eight ball into my eyeball, if that's all it took to drop you.

...That being said, and as you've read, I've been trying to point out the bad in most of us, but I feel compelled to reverse course for a moment. You were a major catalyst to the group that apparently cleaned up the sport. You weren't trying to sell books. You weren't angling to collect a government whistle blower payoff. You weren't trying cover your own ass. You had no hidden agenda. You saw a danger to your husband and others and wanted to put a stop to it. In doing so, you attacked powerful forces head on. For that, the sport and especially the young men and women entering it, owe you a debt of gratitude. If there's a hero in all of this, your emotionally honest self has my vote.

Eddy Merckx, "The Cannibal", never tried to gift a race to a teammate and tested positive for banned substances three times. He is still recognized as the greatest cyclist of all time, and rightly so. He's a beloved figure and a great asset for the sport. The average guy on the street wailing about Armstrong wouldn't know Merckx's history or who he is in the first place. As Jacques Anquetil, five-time Tour de France winner said, "Leave me in peace; everybody takes dope." Fausto Coppi admitted to taking "la bomba" (amphetamines) although at the time it was legal. In all seven of Lance's Tour victories, only one podium finisher (21 finishers), Fernando Escartin, was not tainted by a drug scandal.

The British journalist David Walsh was on the job, and he did it well. It seems clear that Lance put him through hell also. Describing his ordeal, David acts surprised, as if the baby Jesus just fell from the sky into his arms. He couldn't have been so naïve as to think one of the most competitive athletes of our time, armed with a Texas-sized bank balance, would roll over dead for him. As bad as he had it, I temper my sympathy with this thought: often when Armstrong spoke in public regarding victims, it was to raise money for them; often when David Walsh cried victim in public, it sold his books.

Mr. Walsh, you chose to take down a cancer victim well on his way to raising a billion dollars to help his fellow survivors. When Lance stepped down from his Foundation in 2012, the money it had raised helped 2,500,000 cancer patients. Bully for you and your movie deal, David Walsh. If I were asked, "Yes or no, did Lance's end justify his means?", I would suggest first asking that to the souls of the dead who might have suffered less, lived longer, or possibly still be alive had you, Mr. David Walsh, not helped dam the river of funds that was flowing their way. Clearly, you were in your moral right, Mr. Walsh. Although next time you gloat about your victory, consider taking a moment of silence beforehand.

John Lennon. Iconic hero rock star, all-star peacenik,

admitted wife beater, used the N-word as a derogative in a song of his. Recreational drug promoter who put son number one on the top of his lifetime pay no mind list. His worldly solutions were comprised of simplistic ditties and staying in bed to end a war. Lennon left what's now over a half a billion dollars to multimedia artist Yoko Ono. He had an airport named after him and five acres in Central Park dedicated to him. What's Lance recognized for? Certainly not the half billion he raised to aid Cancer victims or playing and dominating the bike racing game the way that almost all the others of his era played it. Sung to the tune of *Imagine*: Imagine no possessions, imagine no five apartments in the Dakota, imagine no customized Rolls Royce, Ferrari, or Mercedes. Imagine all the people, if they could only think for themselves.

To the overflowing stream of people screwing relatives out of money: you were able to pull off your frauds mainly because you found the perfect marks; people who inherently trusted, admired and loved you blindly. They often came back for more, as they didn't have it in them to face the truth of who you really are. Your betrayals in turn prompted you to refine your next skill; convincing others that the innocent victim was wrong or to blame. Hence subtracting them from some family and lessening him or her in the eyes of other members. Within that family, the victim is often defenseless as his moral compass keeps his tongue tied. For this slithering sub species: Frauds and lies, lies and frauds, one is more enjoyable and satisfying than the other. Before you descend to Dante's lowest rung of Hell reserved for traitors to family, please weigh in on Armstrong. It would only be natural for sanctimonious sociopaths to condemn him harsher than others. And the victims can pay it backwards and take their angst out on Armstrong too. Why not? It seems like the thing to do.

Regarding sanctimonious and worse, relax, I'll get to myself, but you'll have to read more stories. Other than trying to make new friends, I guess by now you know where I'm going with this. I've had a lot of bad ideas in my life, fortunately I normally didn't have the initiative or drive to follow through on them. I don't know what happened here. I guess I just had enough.

Widely considered the best American football coach of all time, Bill Belichick of the New England Patriots has been caught cheating more than a few times. The consequences: fined but never docked a single game. American football players who are caught taking steroids for the first time get docked four games out of a seventeen-game season - in a sport where their strength often maims each other for life.

Major League Baseball's all-time single season home run leaders: Barry Bonds, Mark McGwire, and Sammy Sosa. Steroids, steroids and steroids. Not even an asterisk.

We have people who were born men, aided by a scalpel and a slew of drugs, dominating women in women's sports, and we must accept it as fair play or be damned with horrific labels. That's right; they're not cheating, but Armstrong was. I'm normally open to discussion with people who hold a different opinion. In this case, I don't want to be around people who would ask me to suspend reality so they can explain the fairness of this to me.

The good Lance did shouldn't have served as a "get out of jail free card." It didn't. The courts had their say, he paid millions in fines, lost his sponsors, as well as his place in the sport, for now. The public got to vent on who they were programmed to vent on.

Give his victories back to him, or at worst put an asterisk next to them. If the latter is the choice, while they're at it, have that same pipsqueak put one by George

Washington and Thomas Jefferson's names. Washington retired from burning a dozen Indian villages to become a gentleman farmer who cultivated a slave's mouth for teeth to use as his own. Jefferson slept with a sixteen-year-old slave. By the nature of that union, it doesn't appear she was in a good position to say; "Keep walking Tommy". In today's world, if justice were to be served, they would be in jail for arson and pedophilia. Seems like those crimes trump cheating in a bike race. As punishment for the actions of those ex-president's, do we reverse the Declaration of Independence? Do we toss the constitution? If you're still jumping on Armstrong's case, you should consider ceasing to defend POTUS one and three with the different time and place rationalization.

If I ever have the honor of meeting Lance, the only thing I'll ask him will be to gift me a signed picture of him on a couch staring at his seven yellow jerseys after they were supposedly taken away. That's the Michelangelo of FU's to the rigged, corrupt hypocrisy that designated him the everyman fall guy. I'd be proud to hang that photograph on my wall.

What Lance did on the bike was beyond brilliant; what he did for millions of others should never be forgotten.

Disclaimer: All numbers are approximations.

Originally published in a condensed form in Conquista Cycling Quarterly issue # 24

MILES INTO MILESTONES: A BICYCLE FAMILY SAGA

I n 1963 for my eighth birthday, my father brought home a black and white grip shifting Royce Union bicycle from a discount department store. It was a Taiwanese knockoff of an English three-speed. This was well before the top European brands began the massive cross pollination of their steeds in the Asian frame breeding farms. I didn't know the bike's pedigree at the time, and certainly wouldn't have thought less of it if I had. As far as I was concerned Royce Union was the bicycle arm of Rolls Royce.

Two years later, I finally completed New York's Central Park's 6.2-mile loop. In addition to opening my eyes to parts unknown, that bike became the conduit to my initial athletic achievement. Before diminishing the achievement, consider that the half of the pipe extrusion which was not used to build this bike's frame was sold to the Haysham nuclear reactor to safely store radioisotopes. On my best day, I wouldn't sneeze at summiting the 7.5% gradient Harlem hill with the only thing butted on that bike was what sat on it.

Across the street from my grammar school, P.S. 166, was a horse stable called *The Claremont Riding Academy*. After school, I walked over to a perennially smiling guy who sat outside. He wore a fragrance extracted from aged Appaloosa sweat blended with Four Roses whiskey. I negotiated my first business deal with him. I could park my bike alongside the other painted Piebalds for a dollar a week; he never accepted the money. Additionally, I saved myself over a mile of walking to and from school.

Curiosity influenced me to take my bike into the streets north of the park. I soon learned it was an unsafe neighborhood for a ten-year-old. A pair of policemen filled in for my stolen bike and drove me home. We got into the elevator with a psychiatrist neighbor. She asked the cops.

"Was Mitch a bad boy?"

Eight floors later, my mother asked the officers the perfunctory question.

"Is there any chance of recovering the bike?"

The cops only replied with a look that politely questioned her grasp on reality. My father expressed disappointment that I wasn't bruised up fighting for the bike. After I passed along the shrink's instant elevator evaluation to my mother, she travelled down six floors to give the misdiagnosing doc an ad hoc, decibel rich counseling session.

Sometime afterwards, John Kennedy Jr. had his bike stolen in Central Park. No "be serious, lady" expression for Jacqueline. A full court press by the men in blue had the thief surrendering to them a few days later. An awakening to how things really were.

A few years, and stolen Royce Unions later, we moved to the New Jersey Suburbs. Shortly after, *Then Came Bronson,* a TV show about a free spirit roaming the country searching for adventure and the meaning of life, began its

Harley- Davidson-ridden run. At the same time, the movie *Easy Rider* came out. After being flanked on those two sides, my 14-year-old self and my best friend Andy didn't stand a chance.

My first bike in suburbia was a Gold Raleigh Fireball sporting a wooden three speed stick shift with handlebars almost as high as my chin. Raleigh's marketing department must have been a fan of those two shows also, because by the time Andy got around to imitating the big brother he never had, the fireball evolved into the Chopper. He got a black one with 5 on the floor. Our riding goal - like our role models - was not to have one. We'd just go in any given direction until estimating we had just enough time to get home before dark. Subtracting the struggle to hang on to the wheel in front of you, the joys of discovery and adventure are often more pronounced. Without the limitation of skinny tires, we explored golf courses, new towns, old graveyards and the private driveways of mansions.

On one fateful trip we went into a bike shop owned by a well-known race promoter, though before entering we had no idea who he was.

"What do you think of our bikes?"

"They're held together by paint", he said.

He herded us in front of a row of powder blue Falcon San Remos with their flaming red letters, styled as if swept back by the wind. He further unveiled his poorly cloaked sales pitch.

"It would be highly advantageous if you started racing at your age."

Despite smarting from his opinion of our bikes, I couldn't help but appreciate the beauty of the Falcons.

I bought his racing bike pitch, but not his bike. For the next few months, I leafed through a 1970 Raleigh catalogue. A mid-price-range Raleigh Super Course became my target. As my dad had just plunked down the cash for the Fireball, the money for the next bike was mostly coming from me, lawn by mowed lawn. A friend of my father told us the racing crowd bought from a guy with a shop in East Harlem owned by Thomas Avenia. I came home with a white Frejus, Tour de France model with red markings and chromed lower sections on the backstays and fork. When not riding it, the bike was parked in the basement. The water bottle, with its bleeding color rendition of the Tour de France route stayed by my side on the night table.

Andy followed suit at Avenia's and bought an iconic "lizard yellow" (greenish yellow), Legnano, Frejus' sister brand. If you rode a bicycle in the pre-bike boom, 1970's New Jersey you were a nerd. We embraced that. The two of us made a few other nerd friends on our rides.

Our first trip of note was a fall weekend tour in the Berkshire Mountains of Western Connecticut. It was organized by the American Youth Hostel Tour Company. The first night the whole group sat around a fireplace drinking hot chocolate in the lodge's cavernous, stone-walled main room. Andy and I were the only teenagers. For the first time, I was among adults in an extended social situation without my family; they made me feel like I was one of them.

On the next day's ride, we got hit with a surprise snowstorm. For one stretch, I didn't change hand positions because I was enjoying watching my red cloth handlebar tape turn white. I further distracted myself from the pain of the climbs by watching the small wakes and the ensuing tire tracks of those in front of me. Even more vividly I recall miming to smoke a cigarette, and then exhaling foggy air in the direction of anybody who pulled aside me. I said I was made to feel like an adult, not act like one.

That summer Andy's parents and mine signed us up for a six-week, American Youth Hostel trip across the Canadian Rockies. Sam, our adult leader, was a bearded guy riding a bike with all the extra spokes commensurate with his appetite. His caloric requirements were only an issue because there was a finite amount of food awaiting us at each hostel. That food was often kept fresh in icy mountain streams. I better understood the native wild bears' claim to our shares as they had not been paid to limit themselves to an equal portion.

Sam talked about sex a lot. After not abiding by a few of the 15 and 16-year-old girls' repeated requests for him to change the topic, he was removed. I was in awe that my peers could wield that kind of power. The lady they sent to replace him was a better fit for all. Our group was sitting on a floor in a hostel somewhere between Jasper and Banff when the subject turned to bikes. I told the story of the Frejus and that I had paid $152 for it. I rambled on, telling everyone I was thinking of saving up for the over $300 Super Corsa model.

One of the girls asked, "Why do you need that expensive a bike?"

"I don't, I just like to hear myself talk."

The new leader told me I had a way with words and that I should consider being a writer. So, the next letter home likely had my parents thinking I'd found hallucinogenic mushrooms on the side of the road. I described the week's events in pains-giving detail. But one vignette I excluded took place in the woods adjacent to a narrow mountain road. I was on an exploratory jaunt with a girl from another group; she suggested we stop for a rest. Another milestone: call it half crossed.

Six years after college, while living in Houston Texas, I

ran into a group of racers out training. Before speeding away, they told me about an upcoming race and invited me to join their club. I spun around the neighborhood by myself a few times to prepare. On race day, my bike was approaching 13 years old; it had to be at least part the bike's fault! The *Lantern Rouge* winning Frejus was replaced with a new 1983 anthracite grey De Rosa professional model. I sprang for Cinelli bars with integral yellow leather sheathing, and matching saddle. I joined the club and set off on their 60 mile out-and-back training ride. Corky Kobbs a Vietnam-War- hardened veteran was charitable enough to accompany me for the last 30 miles. On the ride, he explained the merits of bringing snacks and eating more than you normally would beforehand.

Other than his kindness and odd name, I remember Corky for one occurrence. We were a pack of about twenty, fanned across most of a narrow rural road. A guy driving a pickup truck came barreling along, blasting his horn, coming close enough to hand us water bottles - except he didn't. Half of our group took one hand off the bars to express their displeasure via sign language. The truck stopped ahead, blocking the road. The driver jumped out grasping a crowbar, which by Texas standards is empty handed.

"I'll beat every one of you scrawny faggots within a half inch of your lives."

"I'm sorry to disappoint you sir, but that would be impossible. Since we've taken up cycling, many of us have switched over to the metric system." Corky responded.

Sprinter-built Corky rolled his bike forward with his hand on the large saddle bag. He calmly unzipped it and reconnected his hidden hand to a prized souvenir from Vietnam. I was ten meters back in the peloton of Guerciottis', Cioccs', deep breaths, and nervous chuckles.

"You think that's funny, mother f*#@&%?" shouted the driver.

"I'm laughing, aren't I? Obviously you don't, so try this one. How's about I bury you in the ground with only your naked ass sticking out, and then using it to park my bike. Now that would be funny." Corky answered.

Like two racers frozen in track stands, they waited for the other to make the first move. Fifteen seconds later, the redneck with his bluff called, slinked back into his truck with barely a muffled macho muttering. In those days it was common to drill out parts to lighten your bike. I doubt the irate driver knew how close he came to having his mood lightened permanently by the same method.

I loved the De Rosa, yet I was made to feel that at 60cm I had bought a bike too big for my 5' 11" height. If only Lance Armstrong and his two sizes too big bicycle had come on the scene sooner. I sold it and bought a white, blue trimmed 57cm Gios Torino. A few years earlier in 1984, on a trip back to NYC, I had invited myself into the warehouse of the US distributor. The owner toured me through the bikes and the real source of his income, espresso machines. He sequestered me in his office to share his enthusiasm for fellow countryman Francesco Moser's recent besting of Eddie Merckx's hour record. In 1986 rather than digging through my shoebox full of business cards and attempting to weasel him into a direct purchase, I bought from a local dealer. The bike came bent and had a sloping fork rather than the famous flat crowned fork with the coins in it. Years later, I learned that bike shop had put me on the bonus plan. Instead of selling me a bike with just fake coins stamped "Gios", they had forgone those in lieu of counterfeiting the whole frame. I should have been clued in by the unnatural whining of the Campy derailleurs that could never be made to accept their bogus big

American cousin. "The Gios that wasn't", moved back to NYC with me. I was fine looping the park with it, and taking it on America's most popular training run, from the boat house in Central Park to Nyack and back.

In 1987 Andy rang out of the blue,

"Do you want to get Mountain Bikes?"

"What are those?"

Andy had developed a hippie streak and as a reader of *Mother Earth News*, he saw them advertised there. We called bike shops all over New York and the surrounding states and finally found a store in Connecticut which stocked a few. He bought a red Ritchey Timber comp - and with the second pick I got the yellow one. We drove out to the country with them 5 or 6 times and rode on hiking trails. It seemed like our secret until a few years later when it became difficult to find a bike shop that sold road bikes. To keep up with the bunny hopping and shock absorbing times, a black carbon Kestrel CX-S, followed by a titanium Moots YBB. When speed became less of an issue a Rolhoff geared, Gates Belt Drive, Van Nicholas Zion. Editorial alert: Speaking of hippies, those that rail against material possessions have clearly never owned a bicycle.

A Central Park rival of mine, and friend I often trained with, knocked on my door to show off his new Carbon Trek. And just like that I was no longer fine with the knockoff Gios. Thus began my ownership of a triple-chain-ring, 1997 titanium Litespeed Classic. It started life at 18.5 pounds. Months later, going down a steep hill, the She-Devil in bike clothing attacked me with the dreaded shimmies. I put her on a diet of better parts, increasing her stability while reducing her weight to slightly less than 17 pounds. That bike and her successor, a 2005 black Colnago C50 claim to fame, were that in 2015 they got traded to an airline pilot for 4 first-class, round-trip tickets, to anywhere in the world. First vacation, my wife to be and I ate plenty of sushi but never made it to a Keirin. Second one, we looped Holland, almost all via bike paths on the Van Nichols Zions we picked up at the factory in Numansdorp.

After the inaugural Royce Union, the first bike I had ever craved was a British racing green Raleigh Superbe, with a key locking fork and dynohub powered lighting system. To my mind, that gadgetry was the closest I could get to an ejector seat and bullet proof shield on James Bond's DB 5. That equation and desire stayed with me for over half of a century. A few years back, Ebay became my Q and handed me the fork keys to an all original, his and her pair, vintage 1971. Admittedly tempted, I swear I never did the tweed and silly cap thing.

The Litespeed and the Colnago were replaced by a titanium Lynskey R440. Lynskey is owned by the family of the same name who started Litespeed. Other sports knocked my hips out of true. At 64, waiting for my second Andy Murray style hip resurfacing, I'm unable to walk more than a few blocks. This is less of a problem than you might imagine because I can still ride pain free for hours. Pedaling relieves some of the soreness. I also knocked my wife's Feng Shui out of true by parking two bikes in the entrance hallway. Every time I come in or out, I look over and… Ahh, you know the feeling.

Originally published in Conquista Cycling Quarterly issue # 23

BATHERS IN BUENOS AIRES'
FOUNTAIN OF YOUTH

T hree or four times a week, I ride my bike to Circuito KDT to train on its car-free track. KDT consists of a 1.3-kilometer, oval cycle route; a velodrome; and a home-cooking-style restaurant that I equate to a ski lodge for cyclists. There's also a bike-storage garage with a skilled mechanic. It's on Salguero between Paseo Alcorta shopping and the river drive. I get there almost exclusively by bike lanes.

During my 5-kilometer journey to KDT, I typically share the bicycle lanes with a motorcyclist with a helmet dangling from his elbow; a twentysomething hipster pedaling with a leash attached to his bike and his dachshund's neck; a chatty couple pedaling side by side in the opposite direction and taking up both lanes; at least one "look ma no hands" genius passing head on at 20 kilometers per hour; a few people choosing to walk on the bike path, seemingly oblivious to the idea behind the little painted bicycles on the ground; and two or three cyclists speaking on the telephone or forced to text because they have DJ-sized headphones on. They all share in common a disdain for the helmet, excepting the aforementioned motorcyclist's elbow.

This path still beats letting one of the million maniacal drivers meld me into the pavement outside the so-called protected area that is the bike lane. The insanity ends when I reach into my jersey pocket and pull out the 10-peso entrance fee and say "Hola, amigos" to the friendly and familiar faces inside the gatehouse. I enjoy the ritual of reaching down to tighten my cycling shoes and turning on my gazillion-function cycle computer. The device and conversation with the other cyclists help divert my attention from the repetitive and none-too-special scenery of the course. KDT, being less than a kilometer from the river, makes it windier than farther inland, so riding in a *peloton* (group) is even more advantageous. Even without a breeze, a cyclist going 33 kilometers per hour is creating and bucking a 33-kilometer-per-hour headwind. The rider behind him, *drafting,* is expending 30 to 40 percent less energy. Typically, riders of equal ability will share the workload by rotating on and off the front. Often, the younger and stronger cyclists will be happy to stay up front and do the *pulling.* My group seeks them out. We all like the sensation of going fast.

Argentina has a strong group of older cyclists called *masters.* Probably it is the Italian bloodlines. Many have been riding and racing all their lives. At fifty-nine, I am the second youngest in an informal group of around twenty-five friends. The majority of the riders are well into their seventies, and four are over eighty. Most are retired or people that make their own work schedules, so we meet there around noon. I have been training on racing bikes consistently since I was fifteen. If I miss more than two weeks, I struggle to keep up with this group. I'm always curious about their ages. Fortunately, they usually ask me mine first. Likely some are interested, but I get the impression that more often their real motivation is to watch the shock spread across my face when they tell me theirs. They have every right to be proud. It has nothing to do with being patronizing; I typically guess they are ten years younger than they are. It's not only the lack of potbellies, but also the way they move and act on, as well as off, the bike. There is no weakness in their voice when they speak. At lunch they move around in their seats and gesture like college kids trying to make their points. They walk with the gait and posture of people a generation younger.

In warmer weather, attractive women often sunbathe on a certain grassy portion of the infield. When my eyeballs are not otherwise occupied in that direction, I notice a few of our group peeking there each and every lap. I think it less a case of nostalgia and more the result of superior circulation. Many have resting heart rates in the fifties and low sixties, more common to athletes in their twenties. They relish relaying their doctor's classification of them as "one in a million" or "freaks of nature."

There is an addictive quality to the audible hum and gentle vibration produced from chains driven by pedals whirling at ninety revolutions per minute, pushing us through the air in unison. We all share that need for self-produced speed. These elder statesmen's addiction to endorphins is no less pronounced than in younger athletes, if not more so. Together we have ridden enough kilometers to circle the globe twice. I have never seen or heard of a crash of anyone in this experienced group. That is even more incredible considering that for most of our kilometers, our front wheels are centimeters from the rear wheels of the bikes ahead of them. If you are properly fitted on the bike, barring a crash, injuries are almost nonexistent. Regardless, everyone in our group wears a helmet.

Rueben is eighty. He pedals with a titanium hip. Granted, Rueben doesn't ride with the faster pelotons these days, but then again, he needs to save some strength for the half a mile he swims in a pool after he gets off the bike. You could not meet a happier person spinning around with the pack. Two years ago in the slow lane, a young, distracted triathlete ran into his rear wheel and knocked him off his bike and onto his mechanical hip. It was clearly the triathlete's fault. Reuben was in the hospital for close to a year, half of that time fighting for his life because of infections. One day, I saw someone else riding his bicycle and feared the worst. I asked around and was told that in fact that was his old bike. He was still alive but had sold the bike because he was homebound. That was then. Now go there on any given Tuesday, Thursday, or Saturday, and you will see him on his new bike with an even a bigger smile on his face.

A guy known as "El Gato," is seventy-eight yet has the spirit and friendliness of a teenager. His bike and equipment date to a past generation; still, he keeps up with everybody without sweating too much into his faded wool jersey. I ride one of the latest high-tech "Ferraris" of bikes, and I often wear out before he does. I asked him why this is. He told me, "Because I never stopped."

Still another friend, Enrique, is seventy-seven; he raced bikes from age fifteen to twenty-four. He stopped because he had to concentrate on work, and then tennis became his leisure sport until he got aced by his knees. I had trouble keeping up with him the other week. Knowing his age, I diagnosed my struggle at that moment of incredulity as not enough air in my tires and not enough oil on my chain, and to a heart problem that must have just arisen. Five years ago, his wife of forty-nine years died, and he found riding a better alternative to staying home. Much heartache can be abated by riding two hours with friends at 70 to 80 percent of your max pulse. Don't go down there looking for Enrique the next three Tuesdays, because he will be in Spain with his new wife following behind the "Vuelta de España," a twenty-one-day stage race.

I hesitate to mention Alfonso only because he is seventy-nine and stronger than me. I average 50 kilometers a training session compared to his 70. When we are riding side by side, I'll often look over and spy his heart monitor. When his is showing 100, mine is typically at a less efficient 115 for the same workload. Alfonso is the owner of an elevator repair company, so I assume he is good at recalibrating electronic devices to his liking. How much different can a heart monitor be from an elevator control panel? Forgive my imagination, but I need something to explain away the painful discrepancy.

Carlos is a soft-spoken seventy-seven-year-old retired economist. He stands 6'3" and is the smoothest peddler there. Call him economy in motion with no sign of retirement on that account. Carlos's posture has not bowed one degree to all his years of battling gravity. One session I asked him if he wanted to practice leading each other out in sprints. He gave me a firm, "No thank you." I then realized he understands his body very well and is all about protecting its engine. He would not want to risk his ticket to health and happiness for a momentary thrill as I was asking him to do. He often tucks in behind my wheel when I jump onto the fastest peloton. I can't remember him ever letting go of it, even at speeds of 40 kilometers per hour. Now that he has figured it out for me, I have stopped risking sprints for the same reason.

My first friend there was another eighty-year-old, also named Reuben Before the bike lanes existed, I used to keep my bike in KDT's garage. I would take a taxi there and synch my riding time with Reuben's so that I could take his cab back home. After two hours of riding, it amazed me how silently and cat-like he jumped in his cab. It encouraged me to bury the grunts and groans that I let out for that task. He was just as quick to jump out of the car, larger-cat-like and not so silently, when challenged by aggressive drivers. Reuben smoked cigarettes until his fifties and raced late into his seventies. Racers are often limited by their lungs' VO2 max (ability to produce oxygen under stress). Reuben was not limited by his lungs for the simple fact that he did not have lungs, he had *a* lung. I liked him a lot even if it annoyed me that he was just as strong as me with just the one. Reuben had a relapse of his cancer and half of the remaining lung was removed. A few months later he was back, albeit not as strong—but no puddy cat either. As I know the excitement of being in a bike race, I don't feel sorry for him; just admiration for the thrilling life he has made for himself.

Francisco trains on a track bike (fixed gear) with only one handbrake, which he also uses to commute. Francisco is one of the most fascinating ones to watch because he is approaching eighty and can keep up with the group at 35 to 40 kilometers per hour on his mono-geared jalopy. He is not usually the first to drop off. Francisco was gone for a few months. One evening as I was having dinner in the neighborhood of Las Cañitas, I saw him with his arm in a sling. He was working as a *trapito* (car parking guide who works for tips). I went over and we spoke. He assured me he would come back from his crash, and he did a month later. Now I have not seen him for a few months again, but I would be surprised if he did not return.

These people are not the exception; they are the norm for this clique. There are also many other people their age who just cruise around leisurely, clearly happy to be doing so.

This group proves that the Great Cyclist in the Sky is open to my athletic input and thus might be somewhat flexible deciding the final day of my "Vuelta de Earth." You don't necessarily have to get old at any appointed time. If not for these forever-young inspirational friends, I likely would not have gotten married this year for the first time at age fifty-nine. Please give me a couple of years before I decide whether to thank them or cut their brake cables.

Originally published in Conquista Cycling Quarterly issue # 22

TWO DRAMAS ON MY WAY TO HELL

Preface to the Plays

L ying should be accepted as a virtue, and liars admired. We should think of lies as nothing worse than non-chemical mood elevators. If the truth is not acceptable or isn't working, simply don't accept it or use it. If there were no truth to start with, then there would be no need to fight over everybody's self-interested interpretation of this supposed one almighty goal. Lies are never all good, nor all bad. It is the act of fighting them and attaching stigma that promotes hostility and more lies, good or bad. Our country's productivity would multiply if individuals and corporations hadn't the need to defend their first lie, spawning the time-killing, inevitable chain reaction of lies. Instead of spending half the day worrying if you are being lied to, spend it more positively. *My husband is a brilliant liar. Why he received a promotion just last week because of that!*

The shame and guilt placed on lies is where the damage is done. As humans realistic about our own nature, we will have a much safer go of it banking on the lie. The lie is a far easier thing to determine. Additionally, the great majority of us are more natural, practiced, and skilled at it.

One lie that would, unfortunately, come to an end is the claim by almost everyone as to how honest they are. I would miss the sanctimonious comedy of those testimonials greatly. *I would never lie to you, darling*, the most blatant of all lies, relegated to the joke it really is. *The lying bastard* or *that dishonest bitch* would be words of the past.

The lost billions in the failing war on drugs pales in comparison to the wasted trillions combating the undefeatable lie. Approval of the fib would eliminate lawyers and the court system. Removing the evil from all lies would, in turn, remove the politicians' main method of disappointing their constituents. As another pleasant by-product, removing the negative associated with the lie would free up space on people's individual guilt quota for more enjoyable sins.

It is with that understanding that you may share in my dealings with Jessica. If our society's rules allowed me to lie at will, we might be able to have a little fun, maybe even end up happy together. I would have unlimited guilt-free out clauses, as would she.

But I love you so much!

I love you too sweetie, but twelve doctors told me I would certainly die of an unnamed rare disease if I look at you again.

Act I

There are many reasons to like Jessica. I enjoy her company. Her personality suits me. For the other criteria that make men stare, and use less brains in selecting certain mates, I am not interested in being her boyfriend. Call it perceived chemical incongruencies. Many people would like her for all the reasons.

She has been chasing me hard for the past few months. When I take my dogs to the park for their morning walk, she's usually out there with her dog. She stands close; her signals are flattering. I don't want to lead her on. Nor do I want to put my feelings into words for her—a speech that I would find demeaning (no matter how cleverly disguised) if our positions were reversed. It is within the above parameters that we have become friends.

We meet for brunch now and then. We go to the movies regularly. She cooks dinner for me. I have heard the details of her mother's cancer, which only Jessica does not see as terminal. She has a terrific career and owns a beautiful apartment. Many would think of her as a fine catch.

So, for my next physical encounter, I chose someone else named Lucy. Lucy is not nearly as intelligent. Two assets Lucy does posses to ease the quick exit I have in mind are the following: She is self absorbed and unpleasant. Another direct advantage she has over Jessica is that she does not live on the same block as me.

The first day after using Lucy, I run into Jessica in the park. She tells me of her mother being rushed to the hospital for treatment. I sympathize, although only between bouts of screaming for my dogs to stay within a comfortable distance. When one strays too far, the conversation of her mother ends and she focuses all her energy on helping me find my dog. She looks for ten minutes, five minutes past when she normally goes to work. When I get the dog back, we begin to leave the park, still talking about my beloved mutt. At the exit and street crossing, we run into Lucy! Ask anyone that lives here. There is not a smaller town in this country than New York. After taking a moment to remember what language I speak, I introduce the two of them. However, I don't speak it well enough to hide the reality of the present situation from either of them. I solve a moral dilemma in less than two seconds. Jessica is not my pleasure, and I did not ask her to like me that way, at least not much anyhow.

Only eight hours prior, Lucy had skillfully relieved a persistent problem. Today is a new day with that problem only made worse by last night's relief. Turning from Jessica, I asked Lucy, who was three steps away from entering the park, "Are you going to walk your dog in the park?"

It really did not sound like much of a question—more like manufactured noise to break the silence and this ménage à trios, about which I had not fantasized. I said good-bye to Jessica. In the split second it took her to turn away, I could see a tear forming. She walked home alone.

My love life has been unreasonably shrunk by my desire not to clobber an innocent, not to mention my own aversion to bruises of that nature. No matter how many times these romantic equations are avoided or factored, I always seem to be left with a walking, talking remainder—and as that remainder gets divided, there begins another pair of crying eyes. I wish I could have told Jessica at that moment, *we are just, uh, practicing! I appreciate and respect you too much to risk the same with you.*

I explained the predicament a little differently to Lucy, who assured me she would have understood if I had crossed the street with Jessica. I believe this particular scratching cat would have had an easier time understanding the collected formulas of Albert Einstein or *War and Peace* in Russian.

I waited, and then tried to make myself feel worse than I did. The thought of my love life being so limited by the obligation to protect others festered within me. I felt a sense of relief and a pride, however perverse, that I was finally looking out for number one in the dating domain. It was just unfortunate that Jessica's mother was so sick at the time.

Act II

Three days later, I left a message on Jessica's answering machine, asking how her mother was doing. She did not respond all week. The following Monday she called and invited me to see a play at Lincoln Center. I thankfully accepted, glad that I was not on the enemies list.

At our pre-theater sushi-fest, I did well to avoid staring at the lovely Japanese girl on the other side of me. I joked to myself that if Jessica spotted this, I could claim I was looking for insider trading information on my order. She's a good enough sport to have laughed grudgingly, had I risked such a not-so-funny crack. Jessica and I enjoy ourselves. I am usually happy around her. I've never been bored with her. I have found few that seem to appreciate my quirks and outlook as much. Rest assured; I am sufficiently male patterned cross-wired so as not to let pure reason influence those sorts of details in my girlfriend selection process.

With Jessica leading, we squeezed our way past two ancient couples on the way to our show seats. As is my custom, I scanned the audience for attractive women. Having found no success there, I consoled myself with the Playbill. My eyes shifted up to the five empty seats in front of us. My wondering of whom was to fill them appeared to be ending as five women hovered in the aisle. My enthusiasm for this performance increased dramatically! I prayed this was not a false alarm. Luck was with me as the youngest and most attractive of the bunch shuffled to the seat in front of me. My guess had her twenty-three, at the most twenty-seven. The rest of her group ranged from thirty through fifty-five.

Had I paid for the ticket, I would have been able to say, *the blonde alone is worth the price of admission.* Her face had character, yet with soft features. She seemed regal, yet with none of the edge and hillbilly haughtiness common to the New York models she surpassed in unguarded attractiveness. Standing in front of her seat, she twisted around toward me; we caught eyes. I could have read her look from the balcony. *What are you doing with her, when I am still alone? Yes, you could have me. We should be the couple.* She then smiled, leaving me wanting to interpret that one expression far more than any forthcoming drama by some dead Russian. I also knew going into this staring contest that I would have to lose, for I had a date. Not only a date but also a friend who had met her monthly quota for my betrayals. More importantly, I was in no mood to witness a scene before the curtain rose.

I believed my hair to be at its perfect length. I was wearing a tight, navy blue cashmere sweater with only thousands of sit-ups underneath. Over that, I had an Italian cut, tweed sport jacket. The stately tradition of a Brit with the flair of an Italian was my goal. I prayed for the opportunity to test these props and myself.

The blonde was wearing a thin, cream-colored sweater and tight-fitting dark pants. I studied the other women trying to get a read on them. I wanted to know if given the chance, would I have one.

I could not make an accurate judgment as to where and how well this pack made their lair. The blonde was holding a suede coat that I had not yet seen on the thousands of high-heeled fashion-sheep indigenous to the sidewalks of Manhattan, but this was only the first cold day. I was hoping she was not in style and had brought this coat and its lovely contents from her small town for the show. I fantasized about importing her back into town for another one, substituting romance for the scrum surrounding her.

She kept her Tony Award-caliber backside at my eye level for a full minute after her friends sat down. In fact, she stood (bending slowly at the waist once, to put her coat down and again for what I hoped was only an imaginary object) before the lights were dimmed. I was flattered by what I hoped were her attentions—even if at that moment, I was prepared to risk hurting Jessica. I like to believe the lie that I would have soon cut off the visual embrace if my target had not. Numerous silent kills have taught me not to appear too hungry while still wearing clothes.

I tried not to think about the odds of this (excuse me) showstopper, still trying to melt me had I not been with another woman. I was thrilled about seeing a Chekov play at Lincoln Center for only the price of dinner. Yet I wanted to play these odds more than I wanted to see the play.

I sat forward with my head in my hands hoping to smell what was underneath her soap and shampoo. With the little blood left remaining to power my brain, I formulated that Jessica would think I was just bored as I inhaled and exhaled deeply. I became tortured not knowing if the scents I picked up had been squeezed out of a French plant or her. Within the first ten minutes of the play, I became painfully aware that pestilence and disease would reign on my family and myself for years if I did not at least give this girl the opportunity to reject me.

With the audience applauding my new idea, coincidentally at the end of a scene, I knew I must give her or slip her a card! As if secretly loading a revolver, I nervously pulled out four business cards from my wallet. I placed a card in both front pants pockets, and one in my breast pocket. The other I stuck in the Playbill. I turned cold, as the card in the Playbill fell not so innocently to the floor. I held my head straight, as I strained my eyes to see if Jessica had noticed. Before taxing my eye muscles further, I decided I didn't want to know. It could only serve as a distraction from the business at hand. I hoped a few deep breaths in the opposite direction of Jessica would ease my tension. I reached and fumbled with the card, placing it back in the Playbill at the top edge of the page where it could be drawn at a moment's notice.

A few minutes later, Jessica grabbed my left hand. My clammy free paw grasped the little magazine and its valuable cargo tightly. I pulled away from Jessica every few minutes to check the card's whereabouts and adjust it. These alignments were cleverly veiled with my pretending to read in the dark.

I felt like I had at age seven during a drawn out and failed first attempt to jump off the high board. I repeatedly brought myself to the point of dropping my card in her lap only to be stopped at the last second by a numbing fear. My muscles braced and relaxed repeatedly to the point of fatigue. Would she know instantly what had landed on her and secretly file it? Would she turn around by reflex? In the same dark I needed for cover, might she mistake it for my ticket and politely hand it back to me? Could I have been wrong about her age? Subsequently would the woman to her right prove to be her mother and recognize me from a television animal show and protect her as loudly and demonstratively as mothers do in the wild? The assorted possible un-happy endings barely held me in check.

After two acts of self-torture, I relegated to watching the lesser drama unfold another forty-four rows in front of the one that had been occupying me. I was anxious for half time and the hopes of a simpler solution in the lobby.

I was trying to convince myself that the expression *life*

imitates art was not meant to be taken too literally. Anton Chekhov's "Ivanov" is about an intelligent, well-meaning guy, who by the overpowering pull of his seemingly normal and ordinary needs and circumstance, manages to get his whole village to hate him, also destroying the life of two noble women who love him in the process. Chekhov sees a fit ending for his turn-of-the-century-play by having the guy blow his own brains out. Ladies, please don't fault Chekhov for being unable to predict the profound and positive effect the gun control lobby would have on me a century later! Nevertheless, I would have preferred a musical parade of tap dancing, farcical idiocy as a backdrop and guide for my own unfolding drama.

As this is not a one-act play, there was to be no quick resolution of my dilemma. Jessica, consciously or unconsciously, tried to ensure this by following me into the lobby at intermission. At last, I saw the opportunity as she headed to her almost lobby-length ladies room waiting line. The quicker I could cut through my short line and finish, the more time I would have to hunt and bag the prey.

When my turn arrived, I pushed hard enough to have carved my name in the porcelain. Although I think it is now clear, I haven't the control over it to guarantee my getting out of this theatre alive, let alone effect typeface with it. I raced towards the door, readying my five-sense radar system to full alert. I was confident I would place the blonde on my crosshairs within moments.

As I burst through the door, so went my bubble. Jessica stood waiting outside of it like a stray dog that had latched itself on to me, with too many bystanders around to kick it away. She had decided her line was too long. Despite not enjoying alcohol, I chugged a plastic glass of overpriced bad red wine. Knowing I don't drink, she looked at me strangely. I took notice of that, looked at her, and stated,

"High cholesterol."

Her look did not change. After realizing it was not going to, I looked away. I felt like having another but could think of no better excuse than, "the blonde."

Act III

Act three produced more of the same. I schemed for a new way to get the little card to her without being noticed. Whatever I came up with, the risks were too great. I now forced myself to focus my plans to coincide with the final curtain. In the tumult of the mass exodus, there had to be a way! Jessica was sitting to my left; the exit was to the right. The blonde's seat was not quite directly in front of me; it was six inches to a foot to the right. We were all close to center stage, back row of the mezzanine. My new stage directions went like this: As soon as I saw the first person in the theater start to leave, I would stand up and encourage that same process in my row. I would gentlemanly guide Jessica in front of me. Then as I walked past the blonde, I would reach back with the card, as if handing off a baton after completing my leg of a relay race. Within minutes, I realized the hand-off segment of that solution was too impersonal. Also, the cowardliness of it might turn her off. I would have to face her for at least a second or two. *If Jessica catches me*, I thought, *so be it. I'll face that, too.* One must often climb the smallest branch to catch the prey.

Anatov shot himself in the head. I didn't have much time to ponder that method of concluding the play. Nor did I have time to fret over the voodooesque sharp pain in my own head! For that shot was my starter pistol to jump into action. I was thankful to the lighting designer for not putting a spot on me, as I stood to applaud before all the dialogue was completed.

Act IV

I was able to take a deep breath. My fighting chance arrived. The blonde and her group seemed in no rush to leave. I lost that breath to many short ones, as the two elderly couples in our row directly to our right barely seemed alive. The row was too narrow to walk by with them seated. Even if I suffered their rickety antique toes through that stunt, they would immediately witness my evil one! Aside from my minimal respect for their four non-moving feet, I feared the following: older people seem to have less fear of butting into your business. It's harder to tell an old person to shut up. It would have been even more difficult to manufacture a credible lie for Jessica as to why I'd interrupted, then threatened to cuff, four octogenarians.

The blonde and her crew shuffled out before us. Unless a miracle occurred in the lobby, the resignation that I was encountering would be permanent. As I walked by her empty seat, I saw what appeared to be a business card. The grade of the theater made it impossible to reach over and grab it. I began to step over without giving a thought to an explanation. My trail leg caught on the back of the seat; I landed in it with a thud. My excitement left only a little room for embarrassment. I stood up, grabbed the little piece of paper, and stuck it in my playbill. I looked up at Jessica, held up my playbill high, and stated, "Almost lost it."

In spite of the magazine in my hand, if Jessica had proclaimed, "You have really lost it all right!" I could not have found an argument.

In the lobby, I removed the little piece of paper from the playbill and realized that it was just her ticket. I stuck it in my pocket, only so I could pull it out later to see how much Jessica had spent on me. Fifty-five dollars was the sum-total of Jessica's Friday night investment in me. After subtracting my purchase of dinner and two cabs, what the hell did I have to feel bad about?

Act V

Three weeks later, having not found an ending to my half of the drama, I shuffled through my desk drawer aimlessly. I came upon her ticket. I noticed for the first time that there was a name on it, *Katie Linden*. This name could belong to any of the five lovely ladies sitting in those seats. *Katie? Mrs. Linden? Or whomever, I hereby request if the heroine of this play is not you, then kindly put this character reference in the right hands.*

Despite the no good I fear it will bring me, and my previously expressed dis-taste for it, if I am not the most truthful guy in town then I don't know who is.

ANATOMY OF A NEW YORK STREET FIGHT

*A*lthough not of the bowing and encouraged idol worshipping variety, a Brazilian jiu-jitsu gym is a bastion of respect. It has to be, as most offensive moves end in either a choke or a joint lock. Your complete trust in your opponent's willingness to obey your signals to stop is a given in sport jiu-jitsu.

When you end up in one of a multitude of finishing holds, you are obligated to either tap your opponent three times or say "tap" to signal surrender. If you are in that predicament and you don't tap, you remove your opponent's moral obligation not to render you unconscious or snap the joint he has trapped. Doesn't take a human behaviorist to know the vast majority of students learn within the first day to swallow their pride and "tap" when put in that situation. That's only the sport variety. The street version, when employed successfully, often ends in carotid artery pressured naps and or an orthopedic surgeon's office. If many of these moves are applied with too much enthusiasm, it is likely the only "taps" heard would be the kind that's played on the bugle, hired by the victim's family.

Ray and Tim parted Brazilian jiu-jitsu class shouting humorous insults until the elevator doors closed.

At 2:42 PM on a mid-August afternoon, they went down the decrepit elevator of the nearly condemned loft building and walked to the corner in search of a cab. Ray was both puzzled and humored by Tim's practice of frantically jumping into the middle of the crowded street, trying to flag one down, as if they were now suddenly in a rush.

The temporary distraction of the sport, renamed involuntary yoga by Ray, was over. Tim resumed feeling the increasing pressure of his musical career not being at a place where it could support him. He was thirty-seven, and despite having graduated from Princeton with honors, he was supporting himself by training people in kickboxing at an upscale gym for Wall Street executives. In the competitive environs of Manhattan, it was tough to find a girlfriend on his salary. He was without that pacifier. He sacrificed a great deal chasing his dream and art. For fun and something Freudian, he fought in Submission-Grappling tournaments and Limited Rules Mixed Martial Art matches. He was less of a black belt in managing his time. He was aware of this as well as of the little time he felt he had left to make something happen with his music.

Tim was six feet tall and weighed about two hundred and twenty-five pounds of not all muscle. Barring rappers and sumo wrestlers, the entertainment business and the fighting world are not arenas that admire or reward fat. This was a daily battle that he was losing on all scorecards. Even going on diets that limited him to eating out of cans could not stop him from regular visits to the ice cream parlor.

Ray was forty-something and in the real estate business with family. They managed small office buildings and warehouse properties. Earlier in the month, a Guatemalan chicken-delivery guy had slammed his bike into their biggest client as he was leaving an Italian restaurant. Arthur K. was the nicest of their clients. For the past fifteen years, he'd accounted for between twenty-seven and thirty-four percent of their income. Now he was dead, and that stream of income was gone. It was diverted away from the brothers, on the advice of the heir's estate lawyers. The new property manager's pockets were a better fit for those lawyers' claws.

Ray knew it was time to get back out and hustle. His conflict lay in the fact that he was so comfortably ensconced in his non-income-producing activities that the task was proving difficult. His ability to sleep was fast becoming limited by a mushrooming credit card debt.

After three years in the sport, Ray tried his jiu-jitsu at a Submission-Grappling tournament. He came home with a key chain-quality medal and a T-shirt, emblazoned with the words North American Submission Grappling Champion. For the sake of the modesty, he knew best—that being false—he called his age category medal, Geezer Gold.

Ray did not have a girlfriend, as he held a constant belief that he was less of the attraction than his cash count. Although that fear was less of a problem recently, he still had not found anyone he trusted. This frustration was the largest reason he'd chosen jiu-jitsu over golf.

Tim and Ray were in a testosterone-driven state created by doses of life's pressures, two hours of controlled violence, and an inborn desire to act stupid. With the knowledge that the cab ride was the last of their playtime, they were acting dopey as if nearing the worm in a bottle of tequila. They comically imitated and slandered a few students from class. They made conversation with the cab driver, awkwardly pronouncing his name as they read it off his hack license. The two of them attempted an imitation of his native accent in the most terrible and high-pitched voices the cab driver had ever heard.

"Where, my friend Singh, is the best place to get curry in Noooo Yok?"

"Singh, my friend, seeing as to how you are driving around all day, my friend, doooh you know where the best looooking women in Noooo Yok are?"

The cab driver sensed that they were only about fun and played along.

"Faw awtentick Indien curry jew ah bettah off in de Queens, day-a-few place in Manhahhtin but die con't affawed dem. Ahhh dee women, Soho aw dee veellage faw shaw."

Ray then asked, "Who are the cheapest bastards, and in what area do you least like to pick up people?"

"Ahh, de Uppuh East Side reeach beeches is fuck-kink worst. Fuck-kink cheepeest, day beech in-do-dared cell-phone dee whole fuck-kink treep an den trow nickels dat me expeckink me do bow my fuck-kink turban trew dee flaw-bawds."

In sympathy with what he was able to translate, Tim said, "I'll bet you were an engineer or a doctor in India, and now you have to put up with all of them."

Under his breath Ray added, "Not to mention jerkoffs like us."

"No, I pooled-e-reeckshaw; deese izzy veery beeg step up forrrt mee!"

Ray and Tim smirked at each other, unsure if this was now Singh's attempt at humor. Then the driver laughed into the rearview mirror, leading them to do the same. Now that Singh was one of the guys, Ray proposed to the still laughing driver, "Singhy baby, I'll double the meter if you get out and pull this cab rickshaw style!"

Before Singh could accept, decline, or negotiate that

proposal, Tim asked Ray, "Hey Ray, why don't you get out and pull this thing by the back of your bankrupt balls? You can hook them to the battery with the jumper cables."

"Uh Tim, I ain't the one eating dog food out of cans. Why don't you get out and sweat off a ton or two before we off-load you?"

The driver ended that discussion by telling them, "Sawrree gendlemen, none dove us con. Vee don't got's de poopeeze bag do attach behind awahh tails. Eats dee fuckkink law!" After Tim translated it to Ray, they nearly shook his cab into the next lane. Ray's only desire for this ride to end was so that he could over tip the humorous driver as a gesture to Singh's sporting nature, as well as his own.

At 2:46 PM, thirty-eight blocks to the north, 198lb Javier Rivera left his office. He threw a sack full of packages and letters over his exercise-inflated shoulder and hopped on his bike, pointing it southward. Javier was employed as a bike messenger. Three years earlier, he had been a boxing champion in the open class of the New York City Golden Gloves. Javier was happy with his job, as far as one can be not working in one's desired career field. He liked the freedom, the exercise value, and the thrill of darting in and out of traffic with his life depending on almost every maneuver. Best of all, he liked the target rich environment the city's streets provided him. They offered him a virtual smorgasbord of people at whom he could scream expletives and fight challenges.

Javier did not have much in the way of a sense of humor. He could count on two fingers the times he'd made someone laugh in the last few months. The first was the bank officer reviewing the loan application to open his own boxing gym. The other was a group of strangers at a movie theater. The movie villain's dialogue went like this: I relished killing your mother and father almost as much as I will killing you. While this line raised the emotions of lots of other viewers, only Javier was moved enough to express his out loud.

"Suuuhhhhweeet." Many people chuckled, albeit nervously.

Javier was well thought of in his community. He was remembered and respected for his boxing accomplishments. When the kids in the neighborhood admired the little gold-plated boxing gloves on his necklace, he felt as grandiose as though he were handing out hundred-dollar bills by letting them hold his hard won prize.

Although he and his girlfriend both knew she was about to leave him, she liked him in many ways. The problem was she did not like him when he also lent her souvenirs from his pugilistic side. Her family, who had thanked God for him at first, now begged their Almighty referee in the sky for the day their daughter would count him out. The fact that they had lost all confidence in him fed his growing hostility. In disregard of their daughter's remodeled face, he had trouble understanding why they did not like him better and take his side more often.

Each day he did not find a manager to sponsor him as a professional boxer was not as difficult as the following day promised to be. You know the bit about time waiting for no man; well, in the boxing business it doesn't travel at a steady enough speed to even let you jump on the ride. Like a city bus, nine out of ten times it only gets further away from you as you chase it.

At 2:52 PM on the same afternoon, Paulie Postigliano squeezed his 262lbs out of a check-cashing joint located on 91st and Amsterdam Avenue. He counted out his remaining $440 and neatly placed them back into his wallet. He then fanned and shuffled his $300 worth of lottery tickets. He always used variations of his deceased mother's birthday for luck. His remaining family and friends were sure to approach him for loans and handouts from the eighteen million bananas he felt likely to win soon. While walking, he practiced out loud all the things he was going to say and do to reward them:

"Look youze fuckin' humps yuh. Where wuz youze when I needed a fuckin' break? Did youze ever lift a fucking fingah to help me? No youze selfish pricks, youze did not. I been bustin' my hump workin' likes a dawg, while youze been getting pedicures, ya lazy cock-suckahs'yuz. Youze want some'a my fuckin' change? Carry my growzuree bags and starts begging like dawgz, I might considerz spring'n fur a burger fur yaz. Oh, so now yuz my fuckin friends, huh? Oh, okay, well let me tell you somp'n. If you wuz dieing in da hospital and needed my greens fur an operation, youze wouldn't do nutin' more den squeal and den dize. Youze broke dicks mooching mothuh fuckahs youze. Really, who is it da fuck dat you tink dat you ares to even approach someone like me directly for da money. Get da fuck out of my sight before I beat the liverz out uh yuz. I'm gonna adds youze fucks to da long list of fucks, youze awares I already busted up."

Paulie didn't tire of his soliloquy at that point, I just assumed you did, if not before.

After swallowing three hot dogs, a quart of beer, and whistling the requisite harassment at a female passerby, he headed back to the construction site on 87th and Amsterdam Avenue. He was employed as a day laborer with a special skill in lifting heavy things. He relished any opportunity to spare the forklift as long as the other guys were watching. He trained with weights five times a week. He also loved the way people looked at him in the gym for his feats with huge weights. To make sure he had everyone's attention as the bar went over his head, he would often roar. After garnering everyone's gaze, he would drop the weights from the extended arms of his 6'4" frame.

Paulie lived in Jersey City, New Jersey. He grew up there, well before it became a hip destination for young professionals who couldn't find or afford space in Manhattan. During Paulie's formative years, Jersey City was better known for gangsters, rundown industrial buildings, and more gangsters. His proudest fashion statement for his trips into Manhattan was a collection of sleeveless white T-shirts. He loved them because they hid none of his chemically enhanced massive biceps and the colorful artwork dug into them.

Watching his corrupt peers and younger brother enjoy the fruits of their labor/crimes motivated him to become a crusader for the "right thing." Or at least what he felt was the right thing. The throngs of fruity punk asses that replaced the types of people he knew growing up on his streets gnawed at him. Everywhere he went, there was no escaping the multitudes, who were not working as hard as he was yet walking in and out of stores to buy expensive, useless junk. It wasn't fair, and it seemed he could rarely do anything about it. When given the chance to right a wrong, he would jump at the opportunity. Paulie relished calling on his only arsenal for the task—his very willing and angry 262lbs.

Ray and Tim's taxi was approaching 86th and Amsterdam Avenue. Ray usually dropped Tim off here. It was one block past where Tim lived, but it was the block where his favorite ice cream vendor was. The car signaled well in advance and began slowly pulling toward the curb. Tim said to Ray, "Thanks for the ride. I'll see and choke you next week."

"I'm gonna miss you…at least more than Singh's shock absorbers will!"

Tim ignored Ray and said to Singh, "Enjoyed meeting you, buddy. Sorry I have to leave you all alone with this escaped lunatic. Good luck."

Tim reached for his wallet. Ray made a face and gestured not to bring it out of his pocket. The cab stopped about two and a half feet from the curb. This was as close as he could get and still leave room for Tim to open his door fully without hitting the parking meter. Tim carefully looked behind him to make sure he would not open the door into pedestrians or bikes that commonly squeeze through tiny openings in the free-for-all that is called New York City.

Three minutes prior, Javier Rivera had taken a detour to attempt to talk with a woman. When it became clear she was not going to respond to his questions, he spent another full block pacing alongside, serenading her with annunciated kisses and other sound effects. Before speeding off at the beginning of the next block, he shouted to her what he mistakenly thought she did for a living. This romantic interlude left him riding the last two blocks toward his first delivery stop against traffic.

One block later, he was still seeing red. Maybe that would explain why he could not decipher the blinking red turn signal of the cab in front of him. Even as Javier noticed the cab was pulling over, he felt he could dart through the vacant space before the door might impede him.

As the opening door was proving him wrong, he screamed, "Watch da fuck out."

Tim did not hear this warning until it was too late. Javier squeezed his hands on the handlebars and brake levers as if to crush them. He skidded, coming forward off his saddle, mashing his groin on the top tube. That pressure was relieved when he flew over the handlebars as his bike hit the cab door. He jumped, hopped, and spun with the fancy footwork he was famous for and managed to stay on his feet. He took a few seconds to catch his breath. He then charged, instinctively not crossing his feet during his three strides toward Tim. His body stopped inches from him with his face even closer.

He spat out, "Ju stupid mudafucka, ju chould look where the fuck you're goin' to. I chould fuck you up right here, beesh. Ju know who the fuck I am, beesh? Why don't ju answer me, aren't ju a beesh?"

Before his fights that had referees, Tim would get very tense; oddly, this potentially more dangerous venue had no such effect on him. Javier's assessments and questions instantly rendered his core temperature hotter than the day. You would never know this by the tone of his response. The combined talents of Martin Scorsese, Federico Fellini, and Francis Ford Coppola could not have directed him to a calmer more straightforward response.

"Do you have a problem with me?"

Javier then pushed his chest into Tim's and corrected, "No ju got the problem, mothfu—"

Tim did not even bother to drop the gym bag in his left hand before launching a straight right hand. Javier was so focused on the verbal he barely had time to shift to his left to avoid the punch. It grazed his right ear. When a punch to the head lands flush, the nervous system has a way of making it less painful than you might imagine. It might knock you silly but generally it does not hurt as much as even stubbing your toe or having your earring torn through your ear, as was Javier's now. The distraction was momentary. It served Tim no more than agitating the bull not quite directly in front of him with a picador.

Javier slid further to Tim's right and launched a four-punch combination, landing all of them with none harder than the last—a particularly vicious hook to the body. Tim bent in pain, fortunately mostly at the knees. He still had the sense to keep his vision on Javier and his hands up. This resulted in Javier repositioning his angle of attack. As he did, he noticed the blood dripping from Tim's nose. He paused, and then gyrated his hips while encouraging Tim.

"Blee for me, beesh."

For most people who fight for sport, it is far more nerve-wracking to watch your friend battle than to battle yourself. When you are fighting, it feels as if you are on autopilot. The mechanism is calibrated with your past training, instinctive physical aggression, and focus on the opponent. More simply, you arc too otherwise occupied to worry. As a spectator, your engines are all revved up to fight but it only boils down to you against your vocal cords. It's something of a helpless feeling. This was especially true for Ray. He was unable to open his door, as there was a constant stream of cars coming from behind. As he slid over to open the curbside door, he felt the weight of Tim's back against it. He did not scream at Tim to get off it, as he feared it would distract Tim's attention from where it was desperately needed.

Javier moved in for the final kill: He fired a left jab followed by a right that borrowed from every other part of his body for power. The jab caught Tim flush, snapping his head to an ugly angle. He stumbled back the half-step he had moved from the car door, instantly assessing the lack of future in this style of engagement. He barely ducked the right that would have permitted Javier to resume delivering his envelopes and packages.

Tim continued ducking until he was three feet lower than he needed to be to avoid the punches. Javier's momentum carried him forward to where his knees were at the level of Tim's face. Still dazed, Tim wrapped his arms around Javier's legs to hold on. Tim's naked right knee lowered and dragged along the pavement, as Javier pulled backward. Javier, feeling he might trip if he continued moving backward with his legs trapped, stopped and began dropping punches on Tim's back. Javier's body was not positioned where he could get much weight behind those punches. He continued throwing them even as they had little effect.

As Tim recovered from the punches that did have an effect, his grip around Javier's legs strengthened. To the crowd of twenty that had stopped to witness this, it seemed that this was now the worst of Tim's beating. To Ray, who had just been able to get out of the door, it appeared like Javier was now in a very dangerous predicament. He prayed Tim had enough left to realize this.

Before Ray could think to shout "double leg," or come forward himself, Tim lifted his right knee off the ground. He was now crouching directly underneath Javier. He sprung to his feet, hoisting Javier skyward on his shoulder. From the leverage point Tim had, it felt as if he were lifting a baby. Before Tim would return him to Earth, he pushed his head into Javier's torso while simultaneously lowering his grip further down Javier's legs. He then lifted them even higher. These maneuvers pointed Javier headlong to hell. Tim's raw strength and great anger formed a partnership with gravity as they pile-drove Javier (excepting his two dangling miniature gold-plated boxing gloves) headfirst into concrete.

Javier instinctively reached his hands out to brace the fall. In an instant, his right cheekbone relieved his broken right wrist in absorbing the crash. Even Ray winced at the sound of the contact. Javier curled up, half-conscious, alongside one gold tooth and three of his native ones now swimming in a pool of blood on the sidewalk.

As a testament to his conditioning and toughness, Javier was almost immediately back to a more alert state. He rose to one knee. He knew he was hurt. By instinct, he was going to stay down until the count reached eight of the allotted ten. This is a move used by many experienced boxers when knocked down or wobbled, to gather their wits before standing and continuing the fight.

I would not take a bet as to whether the average guy can spell Marquise de Queensbury (the gentlemen who wrote the rules for boxing inside a ring). But here's one I'd bet the house on: If that average guy is scrapping outside of a boxing ring and he chooses to lean on the boxing rule book set forth by the Marquise, the guy will most certainly learn or relearn how to spell doom—as in his own. And before Javier's internal clock had reached only two, Tim had jumped on him, sitting most of his weight on Javier's chest. It was from this vantage point that Tim felt comfortable resuming the boxing match. Reverting to his own rulebook, he thought how unfair it would be to put his own knuckles and wrists in harm's way. Hence, he put all his force into a series of elbow strikes democratically spread-out all-over Javier's face.

The growing crowd at this busy intersection began screaming at Tim to stop—tougher looking pairs of younger ones aggressively so. Ray was standing directly over his friend and the new victim. He turned his head often to find where the loudest voices were coming from. He warned them to exercise their primal instincts and fears in strictly a vicarious method. To affect those thoughts he yelled, "Get the fuck out of here—start walking! Mind your fucking business; this is New York—that should come naturally!" Ray remembered what a friend had once only half jokingly told him: "You got to kick everyone when they are down; if you don't, they will get up and get you. I even kick my friends when they're down, before they ever have a chance to turn on me!"

Ray's witnessing of the course this fight had taken, and his fear of lawsuits were the only things that had stopped his anxious feet from stomping Javier deeper into the pavement. Tim was lost in the process of his task and heard little of the crowd's gasping concerns. At a certain point, roughly ten seconds after rendering Javier unconscious, he stopped throwing his elbows. This was five full seconds after the certain part of Tim's brain that allocates mercy had ordered the rest of his body to quit. He stood up, looked at no one, and walked down 86th street toward Columbus Avenue. He did not walk slowly, yet not fast enough to avoid the pain of passing the ice cream shop he felt safer to skip this day.

In all the excitement and with little thought, Ray jumped back into the cab, all the while looking at Javier regaining his consciousness and moaning on the ground. Javier looked back to the source of his pain, the yellow taxi, and cried, "Ju could have killed somebody."

Ray looked at him and happily nodded agreement, and then pointed out, "The day is still young."

Javier continued pulling out of the nap. He began to inventory his injuries and feel the immense pain of them. He looked up into the shocked and pitying faces of the people staring at him. What was left of his focus came to rest on a twelve-year-old girl sobbing at the sight of him. He looked away, put his face in his hands, and made her the quieter half of a duet.

The light changed, yet the cab did not move. This skipped Ray's notice, as he was still monitoring Javier. Finally, as the light changed again, he turned and said, "Hey

Singh, let's get out of here."

Before finishing the order, Ray realized there were three people standing in front of the cab, intentionally blocking it. He climbed out of his door and four other people were standing in front of it.

He surveyed this pack of fickle do-gooders and said, "Don't look at me; I don't know that crazy motherfucker. I was getting into a cab downtown and this monster jumps in ahead of me. I asked him if we could share it and he screamed, 'Get in then!' What the hell would you do?" Oddly, that blanked the faces of this group enough for Ray to push his way through unabated. As Tim had, he also walked up 86th street toward Columbus Avenue.

From across the street, Paulie Postigliano saw the crowd formed around Javier offering their assistance and shouting into their cell phones at whoever was answering at 911. He picked up the scent of the trouble he so craved. He loosened his arms in preparation as he crossed the street to take charge of the scene. He looked at Javier, then the crowd, aching to smash someone's mouth. He shouted, "Who'da fuck did dis?"

His tone and the physical spectacle that he was intimidated the majority of them to just look away. The others, who otherwise might have gotten involved, were not encouraged by his manner to come forward. Most started to walk away. Paulie felt his opportunity slipping. He tried another tack.

"Please, will one of youze just let me knowze who done dis crime, so's I can bring dem tooz the atariteeze. Look at dat poor bastid; youze got a civic duteeze to help." Paulie noticed two teenagers whispering to each other. He immediately jumped over to them and back to his original methodology by asking, "What's the big fuckin' secret heah? I repeats, what's da fuckin' secret heah?"

The one of the two better stocked in street smarts looked at him and said, "Nothing, sir. Two guys did it and ran off. I swear we didn't see which way they went."

Paulie grabbed them both by the arms, looked at the silent one, and stated, "I tink yuh friends a fuckin' liah; woise den dat, I tink he could get you hurt."

From the mouth out, their bodies froze in a fear that was not to completely thaw for three days.

"Maybe it wuz youze tooze dat done it. Youze gang banging little criminalized pricks yuz." Sensing more blood and a miscarriage of justice, a seventy-year-old retiree pointed up 86th street. Before the man's words could collaborate with his finger, Paulie was in a full gallop. Five seconds later, Paulie turned back and asked, "What did dey looks like?"

From what now appeared to be a safer distance a fat woman shouted, "One was kinda heavyset and he was wearing shorts, but he left a while ago. The other had on a white T-shirt, and he was six feet and maybe a 180 or 190lbs. He just left."

Paulie took the cue and now sprinted up the street. Ray was probably a few hundred yards ahead of him. A few seconds later, Ray heard a police car's siren speeding to a burglary on 105th street. Not having the luxury of a police scanner on his person, he ducked into the first door he spotted, Moishe's Deli. This was the first place Ray would go on the lamb—or now more accurately, kosher lamb.

He walked to the last booth in the back of the long, narrow, and empty restaurant. And he took the bench facing away from the front window. He was now staring at thirty-four-year-old paneling decorated with only a small watercolor picture of the Wailing Wall in Jerusalem. The owner's son had painted it; the little man had made it for his father in return for having been taken to Israel for his

Bar Mitzvah. The picture was dated 1974.

The owner's elderly brother-in-law came over and asked, "Yah need a menu?"

Ray was understandably not hungry, yet he felt obligated to order something. By doing so, he felt as if he were Butch Cassidy paying the rent on the "Hole in the Wall" hideout ranch. It was 93 degrees outside, and none of the heavy meats appealed to Ray. Despite not liking cold borscht, he ordered one.

Paulie had already run almost a full block past the restaurant. He had spotted only one person close to Ray's description, and he was walking arm-in-arm with a woman. Just to make sure, he went over and spoke to the guy.

"Youze didn't happen tuh see what happened ovah dare on Amsterdam did youze?" They both looked at him blankly and then the woman asked, "What? Why? What happened?"

He pawed at the air, turned away from them, and then walked off growling, "Ah fuck da boats of youze."

He started back in the direction of Amsterdam, opening the doors of every establishment, scanning the customers, and then asking whomever, "Did youze happen tuh see one or two guys walk in here in da last few minutes or so?" Paulie was making no progress. He feared that if he didn't continue his thoroughness, it would be like the one week he did not purchase his $300 worth of lottery tickets. He suffered for months after that week, convinced that blunder had enabled some "teef" to purchase what would and should have been his winning ticket.

Ray was working on the last of his borscht. The absurdity of the whole afternoon, including being rendered into a fugitive of sorts, made him laugh out loud. While doing so, with the last of the bowl lifted to his mouth, he spilled the Borscht on the front of his white T-shirt. He looked down at the large red stain and laughed even louder at the irony of this potentially damning evidence. The waiter came over and took away the bowl. Ray now thought it best to order Dr. Browns Diet Cream Soda, rather than his usual Black Cherry. His plan was to down the drink, then weave his way toward home. As he got close, he would then call his trusted friend, his building's super, to see if the cops were lying in wait. He wondered if Singh had been questioned, and if so, had he given the cops his address? He then realized that if Singh were still on the scene when the cops got there, they would just grab his fare sheet and simply read off the last address, which would be Ray's.

Ray grimaced again, as he now remembered that in his fleeing haste, he had not paid Singh the fare. He pushed the cold can to his forehead and started to laugh again. What the fuck do I care. I can afford a lawyer. I didn't hit the miserable fuck, and there are probably ten morons that stuck around at the scene to testify to that. When they ask about my supposed and alleged friend, I'll tell the cops the exact same thing I told those fucking dimwit heroes that blocked the cab door. And seeing as the law has nothing on me, I'll laugh in their face like I was the wise guy in a 1940s B gangster movie when doing it. "Hey copper, if blind luck lets you catch him, he swiped my lighter. Now earn the tax dollars I'm a big part of paying you and go fetch it for me, you dopey flatfoot!

As he was laughing to himself, he heard the jingling bells on the door open for the first time since his arrival. He then felt and heard a footstep that would be difficult to describe accurately, as the deli's only scale was not of the Richter variety. He overheard Paulie ask the owner behind the deli counter, "Did youze see—how long ago did dat guy sittin' back dare come in heah?"

"Oy, cchhew knowz? (The cchh sounding like the noise made before someone spits.) Heeze been sit-tink vuh a'vile."

"Youze need to be more specific, buddy."

The owner regularly gave away sandwiches to all the cops in the area. So even though this guy was acting somewhat like one, he knew he wasn't one. Moishe did not need to exercise many of his perception muscles to start detecting an edge to Paulie that he did not like.

"I dun't knows, I vusn't here ven he came int."

Paulie looked at Moishe disdainfully and said, "I'll take cares of dis witout youze help den."

As Paulie stomped his way towards Ray, Moishe pleaded, "Dere's not go-ink to beest any trucchhbles here? I don'ts needz dat kind of tink in my place."

Standing above and to the side of Ray who was still seated, Paulie tapped his shoulder and said, "I gotta a few queschins fur youze."

Ray welcomed the opportunity to test his wits against what he felt sure was a plainclothes police officer. He craned his perennially sore neck over and up and said, "If I can help you in any way, sir, I will."

"Wuz youze just down on da corner of eighty sixt and Amsterdams?"

"No sir, I came from the park."

Ray was the only guy in the place. That coupled with it being such an odd hour for lunch, Paulie was pretty sure he had his guy. Just to be sure of it, he wanted to ascertain the weight and height of his target before destroying it.

"Wise don't youze come outside. I gots more questions faw'yuz out dare."

Ray assumed the "cop" did not have an eyewitness; otherwise, he would have had him along to help identify the suspect. Nevertheless, as there were so many witnesses, it was not unlikely that a few were hovering about who might finger him.

"I swear to you, sir, I did not see anything."

"Just come outside."

"Do you think I did something wrong, sir?"

Paulie did not care too much about the ramifications of an assault charge. He'd had six of them dropped or reduced to misdemeanors over the last four years. Paulie was so proud of that, he often referred to himself as, "da teftlon head banguh." However, he did work close by and did not want to be liable for damages to the restaurant—although, if Ray were to even flinch, he would gladly suspend thinking that far ahead.

Paulie instinctively lied in his effort to get him to stand up by saying, "No youze ain't done nuttin wrong; I would just prefurz we continue dis outside."

Ray felt the longer he stalled, the more all those nosy eyeballs in the street would have time to roll past. Additionally, if this cop had a legal right to get him outside, he would have ordered him to do so already.

"Please, sir, have a seat. I will gladly answer any questions you may have. But I would like to finish my drink."

As if the pastrami scented confines of this Jewish deli were rubbing off on Ray, he scrunched his shoulders up as high and together as they would go, and hand directed Paulie into the booth seat across from him. Paulie shoved the table toward Ray to make room for himself.

He looked straight at Ray and jumped halfway across the table, as he demanded to know, "What da fuck is dat blood doin all ovah youze?"

"Sir, it's not blood, it's borscht."

"Youz'a fuckin' liah!"

"Wait a second, ask the waiter. I ordered cold borscht

soup! It's made from beets! It's red! Ask the waiter! So, I'm a slob, that doesn't make me an axe murderer! Please sir, I showed you no disrespect. I said nothing to you to warrant this type of behavior. I go to work and pay my taxes like every other schnook!"

"See dem fat pepperonis on da wall dare?"

Ray scanned the whole place and saw no pepperonis.

"No, sir, where?"

"Are youze fuckin' stoopid? Or are youze fuckin' wit' me? Right dare above da fuckin' countah!"

"Oh, you mean the salamis. I'm sorry."

"Whateveh da Hebes call dem, but dat ain't da point. Da point is I'm gunna fauze feed all of dem to yuh, true yur'azz!"

"I can afford any lawyer in town! Listen, I have complete respect for you and your job. Yet if you continue this, I will file a report, officer."

"Wudjah cawl me? I ain't no cop, youze stoopid mudafucka you!"

"What?"

At this point, sensing Ray's momentary confusion, Paulie thought, of all things, he might actually outfox his prey by trying to act like the cop Ray had mistaken him for, and threatened, "I'm gunna uhrest youze azz. Get outside!"

Ray looked away. He caught eyes with Moishe, who had slid closer behind the restaurant's long counter to eavesdrop. While shaking his head no, he mouthed, "Heeze no cop, heeze no a cop!"

A lot of things were coming clear to Ray quickly. The most ominous of those was that the overtly hostile lummox directly across from him was not restrained by any professional duty, as he had assumed. Paulie had also caught Moishe's tip-off, and Ray knew it, too.

Ray often walked into the jiu-jitsu gym complaining of

his injuries. He felt all his forty-five years up until he started fighting. He beat many despite being twenty years older than the average student. Other guys would compliment him by telling him he had "old man strength" and "retard strength." He knew that would be almost a non-factor against this gorilla. Jiu-jitsu is not really about strength anyway. The instructors often politely scolded him for relying on power too much. Done properly, it's like a game of speed chess played by masters. The combatants are so familiar with even complex series of moves that they appear only to be reacting. In the effort to win, you move in certain ways to trick your opponent into moving in certain ways that enable you to catch him in a finishing move. In this game, angles and leverage are better allies than strength.

All that being said, Paulie stood up and shouted, "You're a fuckin' dead man!"

Ray launched his first jiu-jitsu move, but only of the verbal kind. "What are you talking about? What problem could you possibly have with me?"

"Youze wouldn't a'taught I wuz a cop unless youze wuz guilty!"

"Of what? What are you talking about? Guilty of what?"

"Da guy down da street. You and yourze friend fucked him up!"

"I'm sorry, but you've got the wrong guy. I'm not a fighter. Look at me—I'm a skinny-legged Jew that lies by pools in Miami. I might haggle here and there, or debate the news in the Times, but I don't fight! Listen, I am very sorry about your friend, I mean that, but I had absolutely nothing to do with whatever you say it is that happened."

Paulie was listening, but his fists were still clenched. Ray felt sure that in order to halt the countdown, he would have to take a risk. He approximated that it had been twenty-five minutes since the fight, and everyone had probably cleared out. Even if they hadn't, if he were outside and the ruse failed, he would have a chance to run.

"Listen, I am more than willing to walk with you to where this took place and you can ask your friend yourself, or anybody else around there, if I am the guy. If I am lying, you can break me into two. But I guarantee they will tell you what I have been telling you. How long ago did this happen? Let's go there now; is that okay?"

Ray pushed more clouds into Paulie's limited reasoning by thinking out loud.

"This city has gotten out of hand. They ought to bring back hanging for creeps that do that kind of thing. Chances are he's still around here waiting to be found, but do you think the cops will bother to look for more than ten minutes? I doubt it!"

Paulie became noticeably confused, and his anger began shifting toward the disappointed kind. Ray stood up slowly, as if his pace itself was asking if it was okay to do so. Paulie jumped ahead of him and, walking sideways, led Ray toward the door. They were about three feet from the door when it jingled again. The retired good Samaritan finger pointer opened the door and aimed it again in Ray's direction.

"You and your other friend should be ashamed of yourselves!"

Before this new clue could make the arduous journey from Paulie's ears to his feet and fists, Ray was in full stride toward the back door. He pushed through empty boxes, knocking over a crate before finding a storeroom door that he mistook for the exit. It was locked. He turned back, took a few steps forward, and braced for the inevitable. As Paulie began to half run half stomp his way over, the sheer force of him stifled Ray's ability to quickly plot a strategy.

Had Ray been able to do so, he might have planned to shoot for a leg as Paulie was coming in. The danger there would be in placing his head at the level of Paulie's knees or shins. The physics of Paulie's approach speed, coupled with his weight banging into Ray's head, would be enough data to formulate that four years of fighting education might not even get to take its first real test.

Had Ray been able to gather his wits to make a plan, he might have thrown a Thai Boxing kick at Paulie's leg to distract or stun him before going for a safer takedown. The danger with that was it would probably have nil effect on Paulie. Or, if Paulie caught the leg with his arms, who's to say he would be kind enough to return it? He would likely reach back to the table, grab the horseradish, and then eat it like a lamb chop with Ray watching.

If Ray had more time to think things over, he might have intentionally fallen to the ground and kicked at Paulie's knees as he came in. If he got past those, he could kick up at his face. If that failed and Paulie pounced on him, he could take him to a position called the Guard, whereby Ray would lie on his own back, wrap his legs around Paulie's waist, and control Paulie's punches by cupping his biceps. In Brazilian jiu-jitsu, being down there is often an advantageous position! Ray knew at least fifteen finishing moves to be initiated from that position. The dangers in the above options were that Paulie might step through or over the kicks, then stomp all his weight on Ray. Or Ray might not wind up in the Guard position, especially with the lack of maneuverability given to the present surrounds. Even if he did take him into his Guard position successfully, with an 80lb and a sixteen-year advantage, Paulie might power and punch his way past any defense, rendering Ray a little too unconscious to attempt an offense.

As he came upon Ray, the overtly aggressive Neanderthal lowered his shoulders and threw his arms out like a middle linebacker about to feast on the quarterback's sternum. Ray, as he'd learned in his first class, instinctively moved to the side. He then outstretched his left elbow and grabbed his own right wrist, forming a hole or a snare just large enough to fit Paulie's head in. As Paulie's head came through, Ray sprawled his own feet back to counter that charge, tightening his grip throughout. Rather than pull Paulie to Guard in this position, where he could use his legs to pull on Paulie's torso and tighten the choke, he brought his legs forward and stood up straight. Paulie was now standing bent forward at the waist with his head still trapped. Ray pulled this snare up and out to the side, arching his back as far as he could for added effectiveness.

It was more by the power of Paulie's own panicked retreat, which forced his throat and carotid artery against Ray's forearm, than Ray's cranking that Paulie finished himself. He started to make a gurgling sound common to those about to go unconscious via a choke. As Paulie fell limp in his arms, Ray began to wonder why this guy had not even attempted the simple defense for this. He held on a few extra seconds for good measure. Ray did not look at the owner on his way out. Moishe had alerted the police five minutes earlier. They entered forty-five seconds after Ray left and six seconds after Paulie woke up. The owner began shouting at the two police officers.

"Listen Marcchhee, listen Jimcchhee, I don't needs none of any of dis! Puts dot Hooligan in a pricchhzzon! Oy, looked vat dot animal dit! Voist he come in here screamink about sump beating up of sump fellah at zuh coinah, zen he startz de'sem trucchhbles vist dis utuh guy just mind-dink heeze beeziness tryink to eatink his Boisht in peace! Oy, vut trocchhble he met!"

Paulie stood up, disoriented and humiliated. It was apparent the little nap had done nothing to improve his mood. The female one of the two officers said, "You, you're coming with us!"

"Youze stupid fucks! I ain't the guy dat done it!"

"Tell that to someone at the station house who gives a damn!"

Paulie shoved her, sending her stumbling to the ground sixteen feet from where he stood. Her partner batted his billy club at Paulie's shin. The female partner got up and joined in clubbing him. It took about three innings worth of swings before Paulie would permit himself to be helped into the back of the car.

Considering all his priors and the current charge of assaulting a police officer, the "Teflon" from the "Teflon Head Banguh" seemed sure to be removed.

Ray continued walking home, blowing telepathic kisses to every instructor and every student that had ever helped him with a move.

Singh had fled the initial crime scene one light change after Ray had walked away. The only things waiting for Ray at home were his dog and a series of panicked phone messages from Tim. He was only worried that Ray had been arrested because of his actions.

Epilogue

In my telling the story of Ray and Tim, they obliged me to forward this: After much thought and discussion about the day's events, they feel substantial guilt for their actions. At 5:12 PM, still that same afternoon, to absolve every bit of that guilt, they agreed on the following statement:

"Singh, we had no intention of skipping the fare. We

wish we had made the effort to learn that jumble of consonants you call a last name so that we could call you. You're a real pal. If we ever see you again, you got a fifty spot from us coming your way."

Ray continued alone. "Moishe, even though I don't normally like borscht, yours was great. I am so sorry about the damages to your place. Even though, as you witnessed, I acted in self-defense, I will gladly reimburse you for the smashed case of gefilte fish. I will also pay the art restorer of your choice to repair and reframe that brilliant watercolor of the Wailing Wall. It could have only been painted by a real genius! I think I saw it crash to the ground in all the tumult?".

BUD'S NOSE

Magenta Lilacs

I t was the first really chilly November night. The kind of cold that had me talking to myself: *Are you freakin' nuts, just a sweater? Who's going to take the dogs out if you get sick?*

For a change of scenery, I was walking my two affectionate mutt-Labs behind the museum of Natural History. The museum sidewalk starts on 77th Street and ends on 81st Street with nothing more than trees, hexagonal paving stones, and a few park benches. We were headed uptown toward my apartment a few blocks away. The hounds on the lower end of the leashes were all the more spirited to have a night their coats were bred for. As if trained to do so, they spotted a woman seated on the last bench.

I thought, with a smirk, *Earn your Alpo, bitches!*

As there was little light, it was only when I was about fifteen feet away that I could notice she was sobbing. Despite the lack of illumination, her being seated and face contorted, it was clear she was beautiful. I guessed in her mid-thirties. She briefly looked up, as one should in most big cities at night. Out of respect, I pretended not to catch her glance. I decided to continue walking and pass at the same distance from her. By not altering my course away, I hoped it might save her further embarrassment. As the dogs pulled me a step toward her, I took a whiff of an aroma more lovely than any applied scent could offer. Ten feet past her, I turned around and let go of the dogs' leashes and asked them loud enough so she could hear me, "Who's that, who's that?"

It appeared as if their wagging tails propelled them over to her. I only turned my head back for a second to make sure she was accepting of the sloppy friendship they were offering. I continued walking alone to the corner of 81st Street another fifty feet away. At that point, I felt it unobtrusive enough to sneak a peek. As she was petting both, the dogs in turn were exceeding their monthly requirement for salt intake. I started writing the script in my head if she were to thank me. After roughly a minute as the dogs were making their way back to me, on cue she said, "Thanks."

I edited out my New York–bred response. (*No, thank you; they needed it more than you, because I am more of a cold-hearted bastard than the guy that motivated you to be crying in the street this frozen night.*) Instead, I went with, "I had nothing to do with it, that was Bud and Rosy's doing." And after a scripted pause, "Wait there. I'll go home and get my Saint Bernard. He's got a small keg of brandy."

I was not close enough to see if she smiled or mimed a chuckle, but I did see her stand before saying in such a sweet voice that it must have had a smile behind it, "Thank you, Bud and Rosy."

I believe I saw her blow us all a kiss.

Bud's instincts had him tugging on the leash to get back to her. The hound on the other end of his leash fought the same urge; I pulled it the other way. Back in the apartment, he stayed by the door for a few seconds with his nose in the air.

I assumed if it were a death in the family, she would not have taken her grief outside. I was betting the cause of her pain was related to a guy who had her fleeing to a frozen bench at eleven o'clock on a weeknight. At the first sight of her, I had felt a stab of her grief. In the following minutes, I looked at the scene as not much more than a well-played hand by me. Maybe it would have been cleaner, with less me, if I hadn't added the Saint Bernard bit. Purer still if I had shut my mouth altogether, but hey, I took a shot . . . and a clear long shot it was. Even if it did not pan out, at least I helped abate some of the pain her world was offering that night. As I understand it, dogs are similar to wolves in their DNA, yet it was I who had the desire to howl as I turned on the stove to boil water for tea.

Throughout that month on my evening and night walk, I made it a point to go just a little bit out of my way to that part of the sidewalk. Central Park wasn't going anywhere, but considering her outdoor opera that I had seen, maybe she was. Hopefully the seed I planted would rise and she would show herself before spring. I thought about her a lot. Aside from the good looks and that lovely natural scent, seeing someone in their prime so busted up made a profound imprint. But the walks behind the museum uncovered nothing more than fallen leaves and then snow.

I had visions of her wedding on a pastoral New England estate belonging to her family. She the calmly and serene bride surrounded by hedges of lilacs, with one hundred family members from each side, all so satisfied with this perfect blue-blood union. That incredible day leading to ten years of shared successes and mutual contentment. That followed by her leaving work sick before lunch on a certain Thursday. Opening the apartment door to an image more vulgar than any the foulest of low-budget pornographic video directors could conjure. After drawing that picture, another part of my attraction to her was this: Although lacking in the pedigree I imagined she had, I could not be worse than I figured that guy was. While with all my past girlfriends, I never went with another woman until the relationship was in its death throes. I hope and like to believe that I never brought a woman to that level of distress. Even if only because I let so few relationships get that far. I liked the hunt, but more and more I was avoiding the final act of capture if I saw no long-term possibility. Maybe I was good enough for her.

A Little Bit About Bud and Me

Close to eleven years earlier, a few college girls that I knew while living in Charleston, South Carolina, asked me if I could keep Bud for a few days. I had half an acre of fenced in backyard and agreed. They had been watching him for a few months. One of their boyfriends couldn't keep him anymore because he had moved into an apartment that didn't allow dogs. He was not the most responsible of dog owners, and on a few occasions, Bud had spent time in doggy jail. I had heard the charges were for vagrancy as he had been caught roaming around the College of Charleston campus. As Bud was more intelligent than any dog that I had ever met, perhaps it was truancy that he served his time for. So much for his Dickensian start to life.

The first night, I lifted him into bed with me a few times. On each occasion, he jumped off to lay by the open window. He would stand and raise his nose to it in the hopes of picking up a familiar scent. He whimpered and he cried throughout that night. I continually crawled out of bed to try to comfort him. The next morning, he accepted my invitation to play fetch in the backyard. I kept him at it until near exhaustion. I believe he enjoyed the rare steak I grilled him for dinner more than whatever canned slop the girls had advised me he liked to eat.

The second night in bed, he OK'd a few chest rubs and cuddles and slept at the end of the bed, only going to the window twice for a brief sniff. The next day, I ran him through the basic canine commands in the house. He obeyed instantly. That third night, he crawled from the foot of the bed, like a soldier in the grass, to push his nose into my armpit. He then moved from there to give me a kiss on the mouth. I wasn't too keen on the order he chose for his affections, but I've had girlfriends challenge me even further in the order of things before a kiss.

The girls had told me Bud had never seen a leash. So the next day, I walked "with" him around the neighborhood. He went out of his way to greet other dogs with a wagging tail. After the perfunctory doggy greeting, he was on his way. I thought he was better than them also. If I even dropped my shoulder in one direction, he would change course to follow. The same day, we jumped into the car to go to the beach. Good thing seagulls can fly, because Bud, the thin mutt-Lab, went after them with predator-like speed. I threw a tennis ball in the water, as he crashed through the waves; I had to scream at him not to try to carry it to Wimbledon before bringing it back. When he finally did, he rolled it at my feet, immediately trading glances at me then the water and then back to me.

OK, Bud, chill, I got your command.

When the aquatic events were over, I spotted two kids

around seven with flimsy plastic shovels digging a hole in the sand. As earlier I had noticed a few new holes in the backyard, I thought to ask them if they wanted Bud to lend a paw or two. Their parents smiled and the kids gave me the OK. I put my finger in the hole and encouragingly commanded, "Bud, get it, get it, Bud!"

All of us watched in amazement. In less than a minute I had to call him off the project, I feared the kids would fall in and drown. During the car ride back, I complimented him on all his skills that had amazed me. I am not exactly sure how many of the words he grasped, but he clearly got the point that I was pleased. Back home in the yard, he wanted no part of the garden hose I cleaned him off with. I guessed he understood the negative connotations of the expression *You got hosed.* For the toweling-off part, however, he behaved like he never wanted to end.

That night, Bud fell asleep in my arms. Three weeks of our deepening friendship later, I called the girls and relayed the experiences Bud and I had. I asked them to please either come get the dog or give him to me as I was falling in love. They said they would let me know in a few days. Now it was my turn to lose sleep and point my nose at the phone waiting to hear from them. A few anxious days later they told me that, as they were not allowed to keep a dog in their rented house, he was mine. I promised them that Bud would be well loved and have the best possible life I could give him.

One morning soon thereafter, I walked to the end of the fifty-yard-long driveway and tossed the newspaper a few feet for two practice runs and told Bud to "get the newspaper!"

The following morning, I gave him the same request at the front door. He looked at me inquisitively; I pointed and told him again what I wanted him to do. He ran there and came back with it. Again, I was amazed at his intelligence and relieved that I did not have to walk to the end of the driveway in my bathrobe every morning.

About a year later, someone pulled the same "few days" trick with a cat. Despite him being the only cat I ever heard of that took no interest in personal hygiene, Bud liked him from the get-go. Dice-Cat was always looking to play. About a year later Bud got a little grumpy with him, and then gave me a look that stated clearly, *Is this the best you're going to do for me?*

I searched the paper and saw an ad for a litter of "seven yellow Labrador puppies, 6 weeks with papers, one hundred dollars." I told the couple over the phone, "Bring over all the females and my dog will select one."

The couple "forgot" the puppies' pedigree papers. Bud seemed a little off put by either that or the invasion in his kitchen and ran out of the room. I was left to choose Bud's child bride for this arranged marriage. We suffered through nine months of getting our legs tugged and our possessions stolen before she came into heat. Every dog in the neighborhood either dug under or jumped over our backyard fence to try and have a go.

Get the hell out of my yard, bring flowers next time you mangy mutts!

Disappointingly, Rosy did not appear to share the same attitude. I locked the doggy door to the outside, then the kitchen door and let nature take its course. As wacky a puppy as she still was, was as good a mother as she turned out to be. When the last puppy was given away, she went back to being her old terminator self.

After a few months of running along with Bud to get the paper, she tried to steal his job. Often, they would come back with the paper in both of their mouths. As time went on, they became more competitive for the work, and the paper would come back to me in two sections. By that, I don't mean to infer that Bud would retrieve the sports and Rosy the classifieds.

I had to keep a good grasp on one of their collars each morning to keep the work schedule and newspaper intact. Rosy was twenty pounds heavier, so I planned it so that she would have Sundays.

I had never been to a polo game, so we all jumped in the car to go to Stoney Field. I pulled my car up to the edge of the turf, parked, and let the dogs out to also watch the match already in progress. That was a clear-cut case of poor anticipation on my part. The dogs instinctively started chasing down the chuck. The stampede was another fifteen yards farther away from the chuck than the dogs. Rosy spotted them first and put it in reverse. Bud stayed focused and only heard the horses at the last moment. His instinct had him turn around and hunch into a fighting stance and show his teeth. It could have been a moving train and clearly he would have done the same. In this case, he parted the sea of hoofs and mallets. I hurried them back to the car to leave, made eye contact with no one, and the only polo horse I have seen since has been on a shirt.

I had the desire to move back to New York but hesitated on account of the dogs' welfare. I told my beloved country vet of my trepidations. He responded, "The dogs are happy when they're around you; if you're happy, they will be happier."

Truer words were never spoken, our bond deepened as we spent much more time together in our smaller New York digs. Instead of lying around collecting fleas and barking at dogs that passed the backyard, we were spending hours a day in Central Park on our four walks. During the early morning and the late-night visits, they were allowed off the leash. Without territory coming into play, all the dogs seemed to get along with one another. Almost every friend I made in New York happened while walking them. Thankfully Dice-Cat figured out what a litter box was for without a hitch.

Along the path on our first trip to the lake at the southern end of the park, we came upon an almost sheer thirty-foot cliff. At that moment I had no idea what prompted Bud, but he traversed halfway up it before I thought it safer not to talk him down. Rosy and I raced up the path to catch up with him at the top of it. I looked at him and said, "What were you thinking?"

I assumed the look he returned was meant to state, "It was there."

I looked back at him, with my heart still pounding, and gave him a facial retort, *So was the path, you nut job.*

Time Waits for No Man or Dog

As the dogs got older, I couldn't stop myself from thinking about the next step for them after old age. I could not picture life without them. At fifteen, Bud developed a tumor that made no sense to operate on at his age. He lost a great deal of weight. I needed a break from the gloomy situation in the apartment. I went to see an ex-girlfriend who was living in Arizona. The whole time there, I felt nothing but selfish and weak for abandoning a loved one in need. When I got home, Rosy went howling crazy as usual, but Bud just lay on his bed barely looking up at me as I walked over to him. I had been gone only five days— clearly he was well enough to get up and say hello. It was the first time I was cognizant of him showing his hurt feelings. Rather than get down and make a fuss over him, I bent down to kiss the top of his head, and then I patted it a few times. I walked a few feet away, turned on the television, and sat down on the floor to watch it. A few moments later he walked toward me, but rather than come in front of me so that we could hug and kiss, he did something he had never done before. He walked behind me and pressed his barely shielded ribs as hard as could into my back. It was so forceful it was as if he was trying to push through me. I didn't feel something so familiar as his love and affection; instead, I had the immediate sensation that he was trying to meld his soul into mine. I turned around and hugged and kissed him in a manner one would after being so divinely reminded it would be one of my last chances.

One month later, and two and a half years after the first walk behind the museum, Bud was now stumbling along with three paws in the grave; the tumor on his side was almost half as big as him. As Bud was adopted at approximately two years old, my best guess was that he was approaching sixteen. The block and a half distance to the park was way too far for him in his feeble condition. As I was walking him down the sidewalk in the other direction, I ran into a dog-owning couple I liked a great deal. They saw the limping skeleton that was Bud, and me holding back tears, and said simply, "It's time."

I didn't want those tears to bust out of their cages by acknowledging them with more than a nod. I had my back to the couple when they advised, "Many vets will come to your house to do it."

I waved good-bye with the back of my hand. I knew I had to heed their advice. I thought of my vet in South Carolina and how much I always appreciated his straightforward advice and lack of programmed sympathy. I had phoned him about fourteen months earlier concerning Bud's cancer and he advised, "Get him on steroids; you'll likely get another year out of him."

The first New York vet I tried had an office staff that was trained to make a fuss over everybody's dog as if it were their own. All in a con to make them feel as if their mutt was going to be receiving special care. I was creeped out by that disingenuous behavior, their fees, and rarely getting the same vet twice in their self-described "boutique" of vets.

For the past year, I had used another doggy doc a little farther from the apartment. The dogs hated going to the vet, as I did waving a towel and a plastic bottle of cleaner spray in the hopes of luring one of New York's discriminating cab drivers to take us there. It was Saturday, I left a message with his answering service, and he called me back an hour later. I asked him if he could come over to the apartment to do the deed, as I had been told by the dog-owning couple down the block that Rosy wouldn't wait for Bud to come home if she could see him dead. The vet said he couldn't and did not offer a recommendation past his office hours for Monday.

When I questioned my South Carolina vet over the phone concerning that particular canine cognitive ability he said, "I think you're giving the dog too much credit; take him to who's ever open."

I called a friend across the park on the East side for his vet's address. In the cab ride over, the twenty-nine pounds remaining of the formerly forty-five-pound Bud sat in my lap chest to chest, with his head resting on my shoulder. I only took my lips off the side of his snout and one of my hands off of him to wipe the tears off my face with the towel.

A block and a half away from the new animal clinic, the driver whom I had thanked profusely for picking us up and with whom I had shared the purpose of this trip, turned to me and asked, "Can you get out here so I can continue along Lexington Avenue?"

I barked back, "Take me to the address I gave you."

I paid the fare without any of the large tip I had planned to give him and slammed the door. He screamed, "You promised to clean the car man."

I backed away from the taxi and took a deep breath. As I walked toward the stairs leading down to the clinic, good thing my towel was still clean, the dam broke. Under more normal circumstances, what would have been a pleasant moment walked by in the form of an attractive women. Bud found the strength to lift his head off my shoulder for a sniff. The shifting weight of his movement forced me to counterbalance and look in her direction. As she moved past us, she appeared to hesitate as she heard me talk to my dog. Despite the embarrassment of my tears, however briefly, habit forced me to make eye contact. I quickly returned my focus back to Bud and continued, "It's OK, Bud, my baby."

She walked down the block as I carried Bud downward a farther three steps from his upcoming trip to heaven.

As he had never been to this vet's office before, he showed no fear as we waited in the exam room. As the doctor did his thing, I witnessed my critter family being shattered. I completely lost it in front of the staff. In an effort to not drag them down with me, after twenty seconds, I gathered myself to ask the assistant, "How bad was I, comparatively speaking?"

"About average."

At that moment, as strong as I believed my bond with my dog was, I was assured a lot of other people's attachment to their dog was equal to mine.

I walked up the three stairs from the animal clinic, and although I did not immediately recognize her as the girl that had walked by as I was entering, she was standing on the sidewalk looking at me. She asked, "Are you OK?"

I looked at her, forcing a tiny smile, and replied, "I've seen better days."

I started to cry again. She walked over to me and put her hand on my shoulder. She gave me a soft kiss on the cheek and then used her sleeve to dry my tears. If it were not at that heartfelt moment, I might form the analogy of her sleeve to that of a Zamboni machine. She took a step back and gave me the sweetest smile. I scratched out, "Thank you."

As if correcting, "Thank you and Rosy."

As I tried to figure out where I knew her from, I could see a tear form in her eye, as she tilted her head back and blew a kiss skyward, "And a big one for Bud."

She put her arm over my shoulder and said, "You look like you could use a small keg of brandy."

"It's you. Oh my God, it's you, small-town USA! I went out of my way to walk behind the museum for months afterward and never saw you. If you don't mind me asking, what happened that night that you were so upset? I could never get you and that moment out of my head. I completely understand if it's a private matter?"

"My fifteen-year-old Irish setter Max died the morning before Bud and Rosy came to my rescue. I was staying with a friend for a few days near where you saw me until my apartment a couple of blocks from here became available."

"If you have time for a brandy now, I know a place with outdoor tables near me where Rosy can join us."

"I'd love to."

"Thanks, I would love to learn a little about you and I don't feel like being alone just now."

As we walked toward the corner to catch a cab, I raised my nose a little and asked, "What is that scent you have on?"

She pulled a few flowers from her open bag and handed them to me, "Magenta lilacs."

THE LOST LOTTERY TICKET

T he summer before my senior year of college, as you probably remember, I was working as a doorman at that huge luxury building on the Upper East Side. I was paid to add prestige and security six nights per week from midnight to eight in the morning. Your upcoming marriage to Maureen was foremost in my thoughts. Subsequently, when there was few left requiring help pushing the revolving door, I spent much of my time trying to figure out what I could buy as a gift for your wedding. The trick would be to find one in line with my salary, the importance of the event, and my feelings for you both. Desiring to put more weight on the latter two variables, my resourcefulness was going to be put to the test.

In this building lived an Italian lady as good looking to the eyes of my twenty-year-old self as any forty-something woman could have been. She had left instructions to the management not to let her ex-boyfriend upstairs for any reason. As she told it, he liked to drink and then hit her. It was made clear to all the doormen not to throw him out of the lobby but also not to let him in the elevators down the hallway under any circumstance. The offending guy was in his late fifties and maybe the most well-known living celebrity artist in the city, if not the country. He would pass many hours in the lobby with my partner, and I slouched and sulking in a chair. At first, I felt insulted that he never attempted to make conversation with us. When he finally did, the energy expended to understand his drunken gibberish and then wipe my face made me glad idle chatter didn't appear to be his thing. As the novelty of his fame was wearing off, so went my desire for his presence in the lobby. The extra attention required to make sure he didn't slip past me to the elevators busted into my nap time. The times he tried, I had to block his path and then explain to him that it would be the end of my job if he went upstairs.

He dressed in outfits so ostentatious and kooky that if he did so as a woman you might think he was straight off an overtly avant-garde French runway. One could easily take him for a cartooned caricature of a '70s Hollywood street pimp. When girls my age passed, I also felt my appearance was clown-like in my ill-fitting uniform, but I had the defense of it being demanded by the job, as opposed to a need to make a spectacle of myself. The marketing of his wares left other artists and people with any appreciation for art rating his stature as a painter in similar terms to how I described his costumes. Aside from the lithographs that cheesy divorced guys on the prowl might brag were on their walls, his art could be found on sheets and coffee mugs, and I was sure, for a price, he would come to your house, kneel down with a palette in one hand and small brush in the other, and slap an original on the back of your ball sack.

Then one day, it was with great excitement that quickly turned to anticipation that the incandescent light bulb of the day went off in my head. For a soon-to-be-described favor, I could buzz him in the back door later exonerate myself by claiming to my employers that I did not buzz him in. I would then deduce out loud that he must have walked directly behind people coming in the back door from the garage. *I have to open doors; I can't be watching TV monitors the whole time for people ducking behind other people. What tenant is going to think this ultra-famous guy is up to no good and stop him? I'm sorry I will plant myself in front of that screen when not opening doors from now on.*

Any guilt that I was supposed to feel was eclipsed by the reward I had hoped to negotiate for his entrée. The Italian lady was under no obligation to open her front door anyways. Who in New York City doesn't have a dead bolt? Besides, she was purported to be evil incarnate with an accent and a sheer negligee, and she routinely opened her door with the welcoming nature of both. Inviting the younger porters and doormen inside was one of the pleasures of her tenancy. One guy lost his job as a result of declining a second invite into the two-bedroom, two-and-a-half-bath rabid cougar's lair.

Hence the plan: Instead of the ten dollars the highbrow cheapskate had on prior occasions offered me to risk the two hundred and fifty I was making weekly, all he had to do was lend me ten minutes of his time. I would bring in a small sketch pad, a pen, and a pencil (his choice) to work and have him quickly scratch out his interpretation of you and Maureen standing at the altar, with a little commentary to the effect of, *With love from Mitch.* Signed by him, this would skyrocket the value of the original artwork past what anyone else was likely to gift you. Suddenly, I did not view him under the same critical microscope as before, and as the multitudes of snobs and the jealous did. He should be judged by the art itself and I kind of liked his garish art. I was bouncing around every place I went with pride, thinking how you and Maureen would appreciate such a gift. It would be a gesture so sweet and grand as to be tantamount to having Johnny Fontane sing at Don Corleone's daughter's wedding. You were my best friend since I can remember. You were like family to me.

The part of me that was not packed with that anticipatory honor was slowly filling with fear. When I had seen him interviewed on television, with all the ego draped on and blabbering out of this pompous paintbrush-wielding buffoon, I feared he might be insulted by some young punk doorman's bribe and report me, costing me the job. Consequently, shaming my dad and his friend for leading me to this position . . . The only friend of theirs who really bothered with me after my mom died. Not to mention subtracting the money I needed for my last year of college. If the Italian lady saw charm where I didn't and opened the door for him, I feared his being a sloppy drunk might lead to a bout of either stupid or ingratiating honesty with her as to how he was able to get upstairs. Of course, that would again terminate in the same result for me. By my going rogue doorman with this proposal, he could leverage that against me and force me to let him in whenever he pleased for fear of him ratting me out. Which would only prolong the torture a week or so before my aforementioned obvious ending. My word against his, even without the damning particulars I would have to impart to him to have the drawing customized. That evidence would spell doom. I guess I got overly weighed down with all the imagined negative endings for the criminality of the deal and with my lack of experience in actuating any type of business proposal. In the weeks before I saw him again, notwithstanding the functioning central air, I perspired plenty into my baggy uniform trying to counter the fear with the good I could do for all of us by getting this drawing made. Almost every waking moment was given to measuring the risk and reward of this idea in the spin cycle that had become my mind.

When he finally came in, I watched him stew in his chair for a half hour, not so much for strategy but more to work up the nerve to drop this pitch on him. As you once told me later, and that I took maybe not as anything new but still as sage advice, "Selling works better if they come to you." I was not as smooth as I had hoped to be when impatience got the best of me. I didn't wait for him to approach me; rather, I walked over to where he sat and stuttered out the proposal. As I was finishing, he forced his chin down, simultaneously raising his eyes up to meet mine, in no way pretending to hide the type of smirk that says you are not worth the energy of a laugh. I continued to stand there too nervous to process his message at that moment; his focus never let go of mine as he softly maneuvered his head up at a forty-five-degree angle to mime a chuckle. He was now looking at me as if I were even stupider than I felt for trying this. As I had worked this meeting over in my mind so many times in the last few weeks, and because the hoped-for outcome meant so much to me, I remained standing there waiting for the finality of a vocalization for this blatant rejection. I had to settle for the exaggeratedly slow and smooth single motion of his backhanded gesture motioning me to leave his space.

Fast forward twenty-five years: A week before Maureen's birthday dinner, a female buddy from the block brought me to a party in a huge East Village loft. Considering the locale, the peculiar thing about this gathering was that they weren't trying to sell the things stuck on the walls or the wacky stuff hanging from the ceilings. As if I had been plunked down on the set of a whiskey ad, I struck up a conversation with a woman in her mid-thirties who was better cast for that role than me. She had God-made good reasons from head to toe for me to be thankful she wore her clothes on the tight side. I noticed more of that when sneaking peeks at the mirror behind her. You really can't count on getting away with voyeurism of this nature. As long as you don't go full-tilt blatant, like palming the curves in the reflection, you have to hope they dig it. I guessed 5'10", with straight jet-black shoulder-length hair, light olive skin with natural blue eyes that did not seem to belong but made her look exotic for that same reason. No discernible war paint, I assumed because she was aware she needed none. Now the kicker: to accentuate all that which had my molecules going wild, she wore a form-fitting, toned-down black leather motorcycle-style jacket over a button-down, starched white dress shirt. No distracting accoutrements pinned, painted, or etched onto her that would show she was trying to look like part of one subset or another. She came off warm and natural enough to ease me into being that way, too. However realistic or unrealistic, at the rare times I have met someone that just strikes me as she did, a future that had tempered hope and little direction becomes at that instant a future of perceived happiness and sexual bliss. The past was no longer dominating my thoughts because I was now living almost every moment in the present.

I can't remember much of what we talked about. I do remember her being interesting without seeming to try. Admittedly, the little time spent with her there would have still been stimulating even if the dialogue hadn't been. My biggest worry was if I was good enough for her. I often start out feeling like that and more often than not end up questioning my own cognitive abilities after getting to know the person. Even as compromised as they presently were, my intuitive powers told me this was to be different.

She seemed to be operating on a higher plane from the standard approval checklist I had become weary of running through. Shortly after getting both the cell and home numbers, I used my hounds Benny's and Lilly's needs as an excuse to leave the party early. I didn't want to chance making her feel boxed in. If I were to move on at the party, what excuse could I give her without the risk of seeming condescending? If she were to have taken the initiative to venture elsewhere, how would I have felt watching her conversing with other new guys after it appeared we had made a connection. That early exit also removed the opportunity for me to say something stupid. There would be time enough for that on the first date.

At home that night, farther away from all that captivated me, I spent a little energy looking for red flags in what she had said, and a lot more looking for ones I might have waved for her. Nada, nothing I was cognizant of. Not saying she dug me to the level of my first impressions of her. Just that I proved that I had come off well enough to snag a date I felt was motivated by more than a free meal. I eagerly waited for the Saturday night that we had agreed upon. I felt what I have never said to anyone: I want to get to know you.

Manhattan is comprised of 50 percent single people. I'm guessing the majority of that group; in spite of what many in it might claim, have no greater desire than to avoid being categorized as people who for the most part sleep alone. As I was in that 50 percent, I would vote with that majority that I believe wanted out of it.

Being with someone you have already determined is not the final answer is a compromise that attaches an added dimension to the anxiety particular to loneliness. Compounding that difficulty, the older I got, it increasingly gnawed at me how wrong it was to waste someone else's time. Ironically, the more you have seen of the others, the harder it is to settle on one. The thing is, when you believe you have finally met the right person, all that confused introspection and rationalization is instantly gone. It is replaced by a new and clear understanding. That new perception tells you the reason why you were born and additionally makes you more thankful that you were.

During the week, you called to tell me that you were coming into the city for Maureen's birthday Saturday night to have dinner at a new restaurant. I tried to feel you out and see if I could hook up with you guys at another time to make up for not going, as I had made plans previously. To put it mildly, I didn't receive positive feedback on that idea.

I can't tell you how many times over the years I regretted missing Maureen's cousin's wedding. I knew it meant a lot to her. I hated myself for letting her down. I should have made the attempt. More than twenty-five years later, here's the excuse again. I had been offshore sailing from Miami to New York City for seven days and nights in mostly foul weather. If I said I slept more than three hours per night, it would be a lie. The morning I docked and the day of the wedding, I was at a level of exhaustion that I have never known before or since. It did not feel like tired, it felt more as if I were sick. Regardless, I should have had you pick me up and rested my eyes on the car ride there, to be physically able to lift my eyelids to take in the ceremony and help the cake fork find my mouth.

With that reflection in mind, I knew there was absolutely no way I could skip Maureen's birthday. Bringing a first date to a dinner with buddies is not what the French had in mind when they came up with the term, *savoir faire*. Postponing an already-arranged first date is worse, because no matter how hard you pitch your story, it is, plain and simple, a deal killer. However, you put it, she hears it like this: *You have been relegated to either my second choice or the discard pile for this weekend. I am just one more sensuality-voided, nomadic hard-dick, roaming a city full of social cons and neurotic time-wasters. Yeah, I might be willing to toss you a fuck, if my first choice does not pan out.*

I called and told you (sans the embellishments) of my predicament and that I was going to bring along a date. To dull any competitive instincts on your team's end, I described her as five years older than I guessed and a career woman, which she was. Me bringing a date has been, to say the least, discouraged in your and Maureen's company. I toed the eunuch line to stay tight with you. Thus, I was taking on a low-level dilemma from the get-go. I called the woman and explained to her how much I wanted to see her and that I was sorry for the format of the first get-together. She said she understood and accepted. We agreed to meet for drinks beforehand to lessen the impact of walking in on an established Pack's get together.

A day later you called me back to tell me Maureen said I could come only if was alone. I pleaded with you to ask her to reconsider as I had made this date before hearing anything of her birthday party. This go around, I did not spare you my feelings. I told you how excited I was to meet this woman and that if I un-invited her, I would all but eliminate my chances with her. You called me back and told me even more angrily again that I could not bring a date.

You first, I called the women to try to postpone. I could not find a way to overcome the reality of my absentee backbone. Whatever verbiage I used sounded exactly like what it was: an excuse. Ciao, adios, au revoir, gone, good-bye. It was not for trying, likely over-trying, in that phone call. I just had no rational way to explain away that I was not allowed to bring a date in the presence of you and your wife without making this woman feel she was on the phone with a liar or a wimp. No point trying to sell it along the lines that this dinner would be uncomfortable for her, as we had covered that in the meeting-alone-earlier plan. I could sense through the thin veneer to the deflation in her voice. Her shrouded sense of rejection made it all the worse; it showed she had hopes for me too. A few days later, the next attempt failed, and as I was a virtual stranger, I didn't feel comfortable pursuing it.

I called and told you that I had canceled my date and that I would be there alone. You said you would call me back. An hour later you informed me in a hostile manner that I was now not welcome or wanted at the dinner, even if alone. Obviously, I was not happy with how things turned out for me, but I felt worse for you, as you seemed so stressed being stuck as the middleman during this ordeal. I called you back a few days later to try to make amends. Then you blurted it out. You told me not to worry, and then admitted the only reason I could not bring that date was because Maureen's friend Mary would not come if she was either a third or fifth wheel. The friend had canceled because I did not comply with Maureen's demand to ditch my date soon enough. I was then not needed, and as punishment not wanted. Right or wrong, I always respected your maintaining solidarity with Maureen. I did my best to try to never come between you, even when holding my tongue made me fear I was going to push the teeth out of my mouth with it. I was humbled and thankful that you broke ranks in this instance to do the right thing and tell me that as you did. It took a lot of weight off my shoulders about spoiling her party. I could go back to lamenting my loss.

I always thought back to that admission. I used it as a beacon of hope that you would one day right everything else. It's been so hard to give up on you.

APPLES TO EMPANADAS

I was born and raised on the Upper West Side of Manhattan in the 1960s. That circumstance use to make me think I was better than those who weren't. From my roof, where I played as a kid, I often looked toward the skyscrapers of midtown and thought how fortunate I was to be living in the center of the universe. On returning from summers at camp in Connecticut, when I got close to my apartment, I would take a few strained breaths due to the amount of soot and the particular pollution of my neighborhood. That in turn would trigger a feeling of bliss knowing I was almost home. The city was my nicotine.

As coveted a place to live as many consider it, I was motivated to leave in 2003. Although it had become a safer and cleaner place than the Manhattan I grew up in, it had lost the major portion of what I and many natives considered its soul. The ethnic neighborhoods that I loved to explore as a kid had been almost entirely replaced by one big neighborhood comprised solely of people who could afford it. There are hordes of recent settlers in the mostly different-in-name-only parts of this borough that would tell you otherwise. To judge their opinions fairly, you must consider their limited experience and viewpoint. Eavesdrop on their conversations at restaurants and if it's not about what they are earning or paying for this and that, it's about what somebody else is. (Don't get me wrong, I'm no better. Me is enough of me; I don't need to be around people the likes of me all the time. I am not a self-loathing New Yorker; I'm a New-Yorker-loathing New Yorker.) The characters who I enjoyed listening to while growing up had been replaced with battalions of stroller pushers yapping between texts in coffee bars about the methods, they were employing to make their children as competitive and neurotic as themselves. No easy task. I swore if I heard one more mother brag via a complaint about paying fifty K a year for kindergarten, I would never drink another coffee in public without noise-cancelling headphones.

Valerie, a friend's wife, happened to be in my neighborhood one warm and sunny Saturday with her two-year-old son Mark. We waited and finally got an outside table at . . . call it "Baby Carriage Central Café." Twenty minutes later, Valerie asked me to keep an eye on her kid as she went back inside to the line for a refill. About five seconds into my given task, Mark realized she was gone as I did my stupidity for not offering to go stand in the line for her. That type of screeching is bad enough coming from other people's tables; at mine it was painful.

I continued my foolishness in the form of baby talk, "Awww, c'mon, Mark. She'll be right back. Do you want my cookie?"

Upping the decibel ante: "Whaaa! Whaaa!"

I spotted a couple of noses looking down at me. As if their kids never wailed in public . . . As if I was a party to the birthing of this twenty-five-pound noise machine. Oh, okay, keep staring . . .

Going by seemingly daily media reports at this time in New York's history, it appeared that baby-shaking was in vogue. I spoke loud enough so that every other table could hear me and warned, "Mark, I don't care if we are in a liberal neighborhood, if you don't shut it, I'm going to shake you!"

As a wave of dirty looks and disparaging chatter rolled my way, I surfed on top of it with a satisfying thrill. Only a twenty something black woman laughed. I don't know how funny she thought that odd crack was. I'm guessing she more enjoyed seeing a pack in the wolf's lair of American political correctness collectively punked.

Most cities I know have types of people I don't care for, but more and more I was finding New York's version the most unacceptable of all. I despise its culture of fear, with strangers rarely willing to engage each other in conversation. Granted, there are so many hostile and mentally ill people there that, if not a necessary behavior, it is at least an evolved one. Again, me is enough of the likes of me! Still the, *what's the matter, you short on friends?* vibe that came my way in various innocent schmooze forays over the years pushed me in the direction of a map. In my last year there, I was trying to deny all the above with this thought: *Maybe much of New York was really the same and it was I who had changed by suffering from the realism and cynicism that can come with age.*

At a bakery café I frequented, I ran into a childhood friend's parents whom I hadn't seen in thirty years. They were now in their mid-seventies. John had been a journalist and Rebecca an artist. In the early 1960s, they bought a ten-room apartment on 86th Street and Central Park West when very few people wanted to. Accordingly, they paid very little. They made another wise purchase in a charming weekend cottage on Twin Lakes in Connecticut, also before it became pricey. I would guess at the time, they did not see these so much as financial investments but rather quality-of-life expenditures made on behalf of their family. As we spoke of the people and interesting places we knew in common during our nostalgia fest, it brought me back to the New York I had loved and lost. To age eleven, when we visited friends of theirs in a huge un refurbished loft in SoHo, and how I had felt sorry for those people for their lack of walls and covered ceilings. I remembered seeing my first play at a children's theater in the far East Village when the neighborhood more resembled the Ball Prairie, exchanging tumbleweeds for strewn bricks and broken glass. We discussed our opinions of the changes that the city had seen. In spite of their unacknowledged status as real estate multimillionaires mainly because of those same changes, the only difference in our disapproving sentiments was that they were able to state more of them. I was too young to be outraged when the old Penn Station was torn down. It reassured me to have people I respected and admired parallel my thoughts, even if our chance meeting had turned into an impromptu wake for a city that—the reunion confirmed—was dead to me.

Where to move was the next step. I thought of Miami, Las Vegas, and San Francisco, but not for long. Too hot, too hot, and if I could not handle New Yorkers' rap anymore how could I deal with what passes for conversation in San Francisco? I was getting nowhere trying to think of a place in the United States that held more appeal for me than New York, which held little. I possibly could have found somewhere in the pastoral Berkshires to call home. For that to have worked, I needed a certain fantasy to play out: a woman who could be contented looking at me, books, and trees, and me looking at her, books, and trees all day every day, with maybe just a little Internet porn on the sly. Never found that. Mostly, I found women wanting to look deeper into me all the way to my tax statements.

"I need a classic six off Riverside Drive or Central Park West," a date once told me.

Then let a real estate agent buy you dinner, I thought to myself. *Now that you've priced me out, can I stop wasting your time and you my limited resources?*

The lady's comment in this interview disguised as a date was the final catalyst to my considering homes that needed a passport before a key to enter. Many people I had known had relocated to Europe including my boyhood friend from 86th Street. He worked and settled in Czechoslovakia when it was still commie. Back off, Tail Gunner Joe! After sleeping in barns while selling tractors to farmers, he ended up being part of the Velvet Revolution. I wasn't looking for that much adventure; I was after bang for the buck and women who weren't—most of the time, anyways. Pardon the geographically specific misogynist tangent, but the type of girl who says no before she is even asked does not exist down there. The roundest of dudes can approach a ten, whatever the outcome; he will normally be made to feel better for having done so. A rejection, as most other social interactions, will almost by rule be handled diplomatically and politely.

Twenty-some-odd years earlier, I had considered Buenos Aires as a vacation destination for two reasons: It was called the Paris of South America, and it was dirt cheap. Between hearing that and making my way to a travel agent, it had become expensive again—as in *too* expensive. Forward to 2003: I read that Argentina had bellied up once again, re-rendering the place a bargain. A buddy of mine and I were soon on a plane to the Paris *sans* the nasty, to explore the possibilities. My friend, a world champion bargain hunter, landed in heaven. We were dining in top tier restaurants for around five dollars per meal. *Lomo* is the finest cut of beef. They butcher the cow differently, so there is no direct comparison. Back then, *lomo* for four in a high-end *parrilla* (steak house) cost nineteen dollars, the same as one Kobe beef hotdog I saw on the menu at an old-line New York Steakhouse before leaving. *Lomo* has almost no fat and tastes better than what passes for the best in New York. That con about marbling being good for flavor is only true for people who like the taste of fat and those who "don't know no better," as in Argentine beef. Argentina is the seventh largest land mass in the world with only around forty-three million inhabitants; they can afford to let the cows mow the lawn and not make a high-priced fuss about it.

Buenos Aires inhabitants are, on average, more cosmopolitan and wittier, and they handle stress better, than their New York counterparts. Here's why. Early last century when the Europeans migrated to Buenos Aires, they stayed put. The savior faire and humor that big-city living brings has been ingrained in them for generations. Their counterparts who landed in New York spread themselves to every state. Nowadays it's mostly the smartest and most ambitious of the following generations who return to conquer and proclaim themselves New Yorkers. A fair portion of those newcomers left *nice* back where they came from. They are often mistaken by visitors for the less common and more agreeable native New Yorkers.

Argentines are very polite and curious to learn about you.

"Where are you from?"

"New York, and I'm in the process of moving here."

"Is your job sending you here?"

"No, I just like it here."

Then would come three or four seconds of an incredulous stare, followed by a big smile, "Are you crazy?"

At that time, the Argentine *corralito* was in effect: Argentines were not allowed to withdraw more than the equivalent of a few hundred dollars per month from their own bank accounts while the government was devaluing their savings by roughly 70 percent. Translation: Their government stole 70 percent of their savings. What my inquisitive new Argentine friends failed to understand was that what made a living hell for them rendered me Mr. Big and all that I made go with that. What I failed to understand was a lot.

Buenos Aires is called the Paris of South America for its architecture, even if it's a hodgepodge of all varieties of European styles. I'm a fan. I was walking downtown and saw an old, ornate Italian-looking building that used to house opera people. It now served as a political club. I stuck my nose in and a woman approached.

In my butchered Spanish, I asked, "May I take a look around the lobby?"

In English, "Wait here for a minute."

She came back with a guy who offered to give me a tour. Fifteen minutes later, we got to the members-only restaurant. It was empty except for one table with seven- or eight-men drinking coffee. They were the board of directors. Various Argentine presidents had been brought to power through this club. They signaled me over and asked me where I was from. I told them, and also let them know I was in the process of settling here. They invited me to sit down and have coffee with them. They asked all kinds of questions without being invasive, mainly curious as to why I chose Argentina. I had them chuckling, as I do most Argentines with my banter. If you are a native Spanish speaker and had heard my interpretation of that language, then you would know why. Those guys, like the majority of Argentine men, had the grace and charm of Italian movie stars. The president of the club handed me free tickets to a tango dinner they were having the next week. As a prospective resident, I was highly impressionable to all kindnesses and slights. I could hardly contain my delight with my new social standing. I tried to calculate how many lifetimes I would have had to live for something similar to happen in New York. It's not as if I could vote in their national elections; it was just their way of saying welcome.

I found a real estate agent to plan the next few days for me. She showed me a thirty-three hundred square-foot top-floor apartment in a period art deco building in Palermo. It was in one of the best sections of that neighborhood overlooking Palermo Park, with sole roof rights. On that roof was an in-ground pool. Don't think glorified spittoon, carved in there for marketing purposes. More like something you wouldn't be embarrassed to have in your backyard if you had a half-acre lot. The asking price was a negotiable three hundred thousand dollars. Real estate is generally priced in US dollars, because it would be unrealistic to price it in Argentine pesos. Even a short-term dollar value graph of the peso would resemble an electrocardiogram from a patient with a severe arrhythmia reading the bill of his last US hospital stay.

Next up was another top-floor apartment in the Palacio Estrugamou in a barrio called Retiro. I'm calling it The Dakota of Buenos Aires. It covered thirty-five hundred square feet, not including the chauffer's quarters and storage floor above. It was schlepped brick by brick from France, back when they could afford those extravagances. I wouldn't know if French turn-of-the-century bricks are any better than Argentine ones of that era, but it sure does make for good bragging.

The daughter of the lady whose apartment it was before she died (or who I feared was just lost and wandering around somewhere in it) noticed that I appeared like a serious buyer and commented, "My mother had an old butler who is an excellent cook, and it would make me and my two sisters feel better knowing he still has employment. He sleeps above in the chauffer's quarters, so you will still have three more servants' rooms."

Believing this none too subtle caveat could be a deal breaker: What was she paying him?

"Doing the conversion off the top of my head, I would say around $350 per month."

"Please inform him for me that he has a 20 percent raise starting the minute we shake hands." I chose not to add, *also tell him, if his daughter looks anything like Audrey Hepburn, I can remake a low-budget Sabrina for him.*

On my way back to the hotel, I was trying to conceptualize myself in that place and keep my swelling head in the taxi at the same time. I relished the thought of inviting all my American friends, especially the ones I did not like so much. She was asking 325,000 US dollars. I took the agent's suggestion and offered 300,000. A Spaniard looked it at the next day, and it was adios to me and that palace; he took his own advice and paid the asking price.

Back in New York, I started to get cold feet. I had never heard of anybody moving to South America. The country had just pulled a Chapter 11, welching on the largest debt in the history of the world's nation's deadbeats. As late as the beginning of the 1980s, they were run by a military dictatorship. If I bought an apartment there, could Generalissimo Peron Jr. confiscate it?

In my lobby, I mentioned to a book publisher neighbor that I was looking to move to Buenos Aires. When we crossed paths a few days later, he asked, "Where are you moving to again? Guatemala?" I'm guessing he never had an interest in acquiring the North American rights to Borges.

When I relayed my plans to a young couple in advertising, the guy unloaded his fantasy of moving to a deserted island on me.

I'll be sure to pass on your dream to my eleven million new neighbors.

As an Upper Westsider, if I had told people there that I was moving to London or Paris it would have seemed no more radical than transplanting myself across the park to the Upper East Side. Argentina was incomprehensible, as it was on very few radar screens at that point.

I sold my eleven-hundred-square-foot pre-war New York apartment, put my furniture into storage, and moved into an Internet rental in Buenos Aires. The pictures online had looked much better than my new reality. I tried to analyze myself to ascertain if, by my doing all of this, I had lost my mind. My yellow Lab mix, Rosy, practiced her Spanish and *Evita* impressions off the balcony, and I continued my search for an apartment to purchase. An amigo of a new amigo led me to another apartment to rent while still on my search for one to buy. It was a seven-hundred-square-foot one bedroom in a newer building. Shortly after its construction, somewhere sat half of a mountain with its white innards and black veins exposed, having sacrificed its other half just to jazz up this lobby. It was situated in a high-end neighborhood, half a block from one of the nicest parks. Three buildings down was a palace-turned-museum with all the original furniture and artwork called Museo Nacional de Arte Decorativo. The guard house was converted into a café. Rosy and I often lunched in its garden. She had an inseparable soul mate for the past thirteen years in the form of a cat. He had died of cancer a month before we left New York. A certain day in the garden, Rosy spotted a stray cat. Her tugging enthusiasm convinced me to let go of her leash to see for herself if this was her missing best buddy. Each of three attempts to get close enough to play was met with a hiss and a swipe at her snout. She returned with a sad and confused look on her face, so I gave up a piece of my sandwich to distract her from the disappointment. As she digested her mozzarella and prosciutto, I did the fact that there was no yesterday or turning back.

My seventy-year-old landlord could not have been nicer; he invited me to a non-touristy tango with his buddies. The first time I needed a plumber for a leaky faucet, as a token of my appreciation and largeness, I did not pass on the bill; it came out to less than three dollars. He offered to sell me the place for thirty-four thousand dollars. I fumed to myself: *And where am I supposed to put the butler, in the boiler room? Sorry, no can do. Who is it the fuck do you think that you are to even imagine that I could live like that? The nerve!*

I ended up buying in a turn-of-the-century French building in a neighborhood called Recoleta. Roughly three thousand feet, over-twelve-foot-high ceilings, detailed to the point of making the Metropolitan Museum of Art jealous. Four bedrooms, four and a half baths, but with only two maid's rooms is what I settled on. It was even less expensive than the others. I paid in cash that was counted out at the closing table. That's how it's done. Bad checks and mortgage crises don't exist here because nobody takes checks and banks don't give mortgages. In a certain way, it's better. It keeps people from behaving like they have more than they really do and, thus, makes for less people owned by the company store.

After living here thirteen years I'm still weighing the pluses and the minuses of the move. Waiter service here is not what the First World is used to, but on the other hand, they will never try to push you from the table, even with people waiting. I often eat in the brasserie below my building. One waiter has never been pleasant to me. At a certain lunch and Spanish class, my long-suffering (as long as she has been trying to teach me) tutor Eugenia commented, "I don't think he likes Americans."

Coincidently, when I gave him my order that day, he warned, "That has egg in it."

I am allergic to eggs, and in the thirteen years of eating lunch there on average two times per week, no matter how many times I have mentioned it to the same wait-staff, not once till that day had any of them remembered to warn me. Nope, think again; I tip closer to 15 percent when no Argentine will give more than the customary 10. Nope, I know better than to bark in there. I stood up to shake his hand and say: "Thank you so much for remembering!"

"Well, you have been coming in here for four or five years. I ought to remember."

Correcting, "It will be thirteen years in June."

With little sign of surprise or any other emotion, "Is that so?"

"How long have you been working here?"

"Since nineteen seventy-seven."

I should have figured that one out sooner. Waiters are paid a comparative higher salary and do not rely on tips as heavily as their American counterparts. To fire him, the owner would have to pay him one month's salary for every year he has worked there. By the time of that lunch in May 2015, simple math will tell you he might as well own the place.

Supers of buildings are called *porteros*. They have a strong union, and the same one-month-a-year payoff applies to them as almost all workers in any field. The city is filled with old *porteros* acting like they want to get fired knowing they won't. To get rid of one would require the tenants working together to accomplish it. In this country, that presents a larger problem than Republicans and Democrats compromising for the common good. The upside for service people here, and sometimes both sides in the big picture, is you must establish relationships with and be kind to workers to hope to get good service. As free enterprising Americans, we often just expect service people to behave like smiling trained seals at the rattling of the change in our pockets. The downside here in Argentina is that if, like me, you are not born into their system, it can be exasperating.

My cousin Steven, his wife, and three kids were coming to visit, so I went to the Teatro Colón to purchase tickets. Sorry, nothing in New York can be compared to it. Think pimped-out La Scala or Bolshoi Theater. At the box office, I asked to buy a whole box for the ballet *Swan Lake* for our group of seven.

The young lady in the box office informed me, "The boxes only have six seats."

I said, "No problema. I'll sit in the neighboring box."

The accommodating young woman smiled and said, "No need for that. The usher can put another seat in there."

She printed out seven tickets all marked for the same box. By theater geography, our seats were right about where Lincoln took it to the head. At the entrance to our box, I handed the twenty-five-something woman our tickets and she informed me, "Only six people are permitted per box."

I replied, "The lady who sold me the tickets said it was okay and that you could bring another chair here."

"I'm sorry, only six people in a box. It's the rule."

"I did not buy these tickets in the street. I bought them at your ticket office downstairs, and all seven tickets denote this box. If that's the rule, why did the lady sell them to me all printed with this box's number on it?" She responded with a blank stare. I asked, "Can you please get your supervisor?"

The short and stout fortyish-looking head usher came over, and we repeated the exact same script as above. I demanded that he take me to see the theater manager. Because I had no plans of backing down, I feared this was to become *Swan Song Lake* for our evening's entertainment. The hard bodies were already twirling and jumping in and out of each other's arms. Not that I cared; we were sitting too far away to give me any thrill. In crept just a little pre-show-two-puff-paranoia, as I feared the agitated usher would be tempted to advance my Lincoln analogy if I got to sit in my desired chair. Eventually, I did something Argentines do far more seldom than New Yorkers and raised my voice. The manager gave the usher a give-the-schnook-his-chair nod and jerky hand signal. Five minutes later, as I had my back to the box entrance, the head usher entered and slammed the chair down on the floor of our box; after the sharp noise ringing in the back of my head, I thought I saw him swinging from a rope onto the stage and shouting, "*Sic semper tyrannis, gringo!*"

What I had failed to recognize then was that what they had tried to pull is an accepted method here for them to get their "gratuity." Showing me that they held the power and extorting the "tip" before the service is just their way. Any time I get in a quagmire with a human obstacle, which is too often, I have to realign my mind-set to understand theirs. They might have got the above backward, just like their grammar, but at least they drive on the correct side of the road.

I was stuck in a traffic jam on a street called Riobamba. I needed to cross a large avenue and a major artery leaving downtown called Cordoba. From my starting point to Cordoba, what normally would take a few minutes had become fifteen. When we finally came to Cordoba, I counted fourteen kids between nine and twelve-years old waving signs and blocking traffic that was either trying to turn onto Cordoba or continue on it from the direction of downtown. They were taking pictures of one another with their cell phones, laughing and running around poking one another with their protest signs. There were three police officers protecting them. I could not understand how a country trying to survive in such a competitive world could permit this to happen.

A *porteño* (Buenos Aires native) friend explained it to me this way: "During our dirty war in the late seventies and early eighties, the military government drugged and dropped roughly thirty thousand people into the river. Those people liked to protest in the street, too, albeit a percentage of them also liked to set off bombs. The scars still run deep, so that no organized group—police, politicians, etc.—want to be seen publicly removing people's right to express themselves." *Publicly* is the keyword there, because behind the scenes, they work at it on a full-time basis. A few years ago, the government tried to institute a new law banning books from the United States and Europe because their inks cause cancer. The law did not pass for anything but a message in how far they thought they could go to dupe their public. If I had to think of a good title for the political section of a newspaper here, *Theater of the Absurd* would work. You know how in the United States when people are asked how they are doing, they often answer *Same old, same old?* Argentines don't use that phrase, because it does not apply. Every day is a new adventure.

As a people, if they respect your expert authority at all, it will only last until they feel they can just barely get by without you. It's less about winning as a group and more about the power of the individual. Maybe the banana republic history we thrust on them might have something to do with this. Simply put, they don't want to be subjugated by outsiders.

In New York, every three or four weeks I found someone who might have been telling me the truth. Like for most things, here you wait a little longer. Somewhat understandable when you consider that in many of their lifetimes, telling the truth might have gotten them killed.

Foreigners often find doing business here a death sentence. It's not conducive to business when you mix the above with a people who have no belief in the long term. Why should they? Their populist governments almost as a rule have blown up the economy with hyperinflation and draconian anti-commerce laws enacted to compensate and cover up for their blatant self-interest.

Throughout South America, they are known to be arrogant. I find the opposite. Most everyone you meet will tell you, "We are a screwed-up people." They are forced to accept systemic corruption because that's what exists here. It's the only system most of them have ever known. Frank Sinatra's song for Buenos Aires might have gone like this: *If you can make it in Buenos Aires, eh, uh . . . Now you're talking!* Frank made two million dollars from his five sold-out performances in Buenos Aires in 1981. His Argentine producer, Palito Ortega, thanks to the military government and exchange rates, filed for bankruptcy afterward.

Even though they don't see it, they are far, far ahead of us in social skills and good manners. For whatever reason, as a people they appear so much happier than Americans, let alone New Yorkers.

Some stateside friends ask, "Will you ever come home?"

I am.

YAW WRONG! YAW WRONG! YAW WRONG!

There are at least some advantages in joining a man and a woman together without the complexity of a sexual relationship. Would-be battle lines in a romantic coupling might simply be used as guidelines in a sexless friendship. Having a secret outside agenda in a romantic pairing can often be linked to the throwing of tantrums and the occasional heavy metal object. Confiding certain things in an inter-sex friendship is usually safer than with a lover. The sexless couple views each other's purpose under a weaker microscope, along with a more relaxed view of each other's limitations. I am not trying to argue the benefits of subtracting sexual gratification between men and women; rather, I am trying to place at least some positive perspective on the friendship of Helen and Max within the confines of this family setting.

Helen's high level of intelligence was unique amongst Max's small circle of friends. Her push for a relationship, to which he knew he could not commit, was flattering. In reaching goals outside of her mate procurement domain,

Helen was having more success. Paper, canvas covered cardboard, and those holding them were spit in all directions as she chewed her way through the publishing world. Max not only liked her but also felt good about himself because someone like her would call him a friend.

Helen was without a boyfriend at thirty-five. In spite of career successes, she told Max she could never be happy without a guy in at least that capacity. Max offered up help of this nature: "You're not having a boyfriend would be slightly more acceptable if you had at least a husband."

Family gatherings were difficult for her. Her unhappily married older sister and unemployed married younger brother had two kids apiece. Her mother made regular mention to her of only the matrimonial and child rearing aspects of those facts. Each time, in a slow deliberate tone, as if Helen had just woken from a thirteen-year coma and missed the weddings—

"Ya knows . . . both your sistah…"

Helen only thought, *Mom, enough already. Put that plastic thing back over my face and let me go back to sleep!*

There was no backing off of her brother and sister either. With a certain digit of her left hand stark naked as it was, bitch slapping the collective faces of her family would not have left an impression. There was food, and they were feasting. Although mama buzzard's comments were sometimes better intentioned than those of the siblings, she would not interfere in their coy pecking. She felt that in spite of the pain, it would speed Helen's selection process.

Performing one of his unspoken functions, Max arrived at Helen's sister's home for a holiday dinner exactly at the appointed hour. His host greeted him for the first time with little cheer and some suspicion. Walking towards the kitchen with her back to him, she told Max, "Helen is running an hour late. Go in the living room—everyone else is in there."

Max thought to himself, hmm, should I make myself at home? Should I smile and just go ahead and introduce myself?

He walked into the living room of the large New York apartment. The place was spotted with odd, shaped furniture that would have had sensible people shaking their heads if given the cost of those obtuse pieces. It all too colorfully made those not enamored with artsy furniture aware that no homage or accommodation was given to the original classic style of this circa 1916 home. Even the original African rosewood floor was buried for dead under wall-to-wall salmon-colored carpeting.

Other than the few seconds when being let in, the only time he spent alone with Helen's sister was right before dinner. She showed off the rest of her place and her piles of knickknacks she called, "ann-tick-wit-ees and objects of art collected during my extensive periods overseas."

Max would have liked to ask, what possessed you to purchase, pack, and drag that junk all the way here? I didn't need it to figure out you have no taste. Now hurry up and feed me and let me get the hell out of here.

Her manners were such that his thoughts went without self-judgment. That feeling only left to make room for another equally hostile one.

The "parlor" furniture was supporting five adults with four of the following generation scattered on the floor. After waiting a few moments for someone to make verbal notice, Max introduced himself. To the half of the room that made the effort to reciprocate, he felt thankful. To the other half he also felt thankful for not having to bother with them. Through their banter, he weighed worse ways to spend an hour. A dentist's waiting room with only two trade magazines would not be one of them. The family spoke only amongst themselves. They appeared to him no more than a collection of squeaking and bouncing appendages. Max occupied most of this time looking out of the window at people walking in the street with whom he wished he could trade places.

Twenty minutes later, Max found himself speaking with Helen's sister's older boy. The first short exchange had him looking for a way to give the boy a complex his mother already hadn't. Realizing the futility of the task, he moved to the younger brother, who was lost in his attempt to assemble a Chinese pinball machine called a Pachinko Palace. Max was aware of his own poor mechanical aptitude, and under ordinary circumstances, he would rather have been water tortured by whatever device the Pachinko people have for that. Yet in this moment of monumental boredom, he was glad to trudge through the poorly translated directions.

With most of his newly found patience and thirty minutes having elapsed, he arrived at what he hoped was a completion. Max attempted to flick the device, which if functioning would send a little stainless-steel ball in motion. Before he could complete the test flight, the boy threw all eighty-five pounds of himself between Max and the machine. He whacked Max's hand off the flicker with his foot at the end of the leap. Then he glared at Max and scolded, "You'll get your chance!" He played the machine until forced off by his older brother, who likely saw this half-working, hyper-kinetic contraption as a window into his own mind.

Max's thoughts of flicking the brothers around the room like the little metal balls were interrupted by an overheard point of interest. Helen's mother began chattering about an antique clock. Fueling his enthusiasm was the fact that moments before, Helen had called again to inform everyone that due to work, she was adding another thirty minutes to Max's original sentence. For lack of dental trade magazines, and out of the environmentally induced depression, he blurted to Helen's mother, "I collect antique watches and clocks."

The whole room stopped and looked at him. He hoped it was only because he had not spoken directly to an adult since entering rather than the anticipated pleasure they were hoping to take by his stepping into the arena with their champion. With either mock surprise or simple haughtiness she asked, "Oh do you?"

Regardless of the interpretation, Max realized instantly that he had stepped in with a lion with no exit sign in sight. Sliding forward in her seat, her hands shifting from the armrests to her hips, she then swiveled them to point both forefingers at him as if they were six shooters and continued in a tone that smacked of test.

"Well, let me ask you this then, Mistah Collectah. I have a French clock. A truly stunning piece, you nevah have seen nicer. It's mostly onyx, maybe marble. It's got what I think is Cherry wood around the base. The angels on it are some black metal and the things they are carrying are gold, eighteen carats you can be assured. I can't find the winding key but I doubt that matters—I was guaranteed it works perfect. My mother lived in France you know. I wish she woulda had the smarts to bring some back with her.

"Whatya think it's worth?"

Max, incapable of distinguishing any French clock maker's name from that of a French bidet maker, blundered, "Do you know the name of the maker?"

With great pause, she said she didn't. He exhaled, while praying that her exaggerated squinting and looking at the ceiling would not help her remember it.

Still looking up in the air, she asked again for its value.

He responded with, "It would be hard to say."

Turning back to him, she pressed, "Even a guess? Just about what do you think it's worth?"

"Well, I really only collect American clocks and one particular maker at that, Sessions."

She again asked for a dollar amount. Her face appeared as if he'd misunderstood the question the first time. He remained silent. She now looked at him as if he were stupider than even he thought himself to be just for walking into this room in the first place. Hoping to soften her with a bow to her comparatively higher stature, he said, "French clocks are a little out of my league." Further regrouping and patronizing he continued. "It's to my understanding that French clocks are valued as much by the individual piece as by the builder, as so many of them are one of a kind, like artwork."

First off, lady, just like French women that I've paid to wind with a key harder than the one you lost, most sold here are fakes. Their antique industry is modeled after a process made famous by Henry Ford. Knockoffs cast by modern-day slobs, even too dirty and rude to be accepted as Parisian waiters. Let me also point out they're not big on cherry trees in France. And one of the few things the Frenchies don't brag about is imported. The more valuable of your two guesses, onyx, I can get three times as much of it, sans bargaining, in a thirty-dollar Mexican chess set at any flea market in town. If those angels were holding eighteen-karat gold harps, arrows, or their eyes after you became the owner, they would have already melted them down and sold them to buy their way off that fraudulent junk you call a clock. Whether a kook like yourself stumbled onto the real McCoy or a fake you'd safer bank on, I don't care. Either way, I estimate the value of your work of art a bargain at two point six million dollars, predicated on one thing: It chimes on the minute. Party over. Time to go home!

To his spoken words she responded, "That's nice to know because I think the one I got is something very special—very, very special. Let me ask you this then, collectah man. I've got a Bulova watch from the Fifties.

"Whatya think that's worth?"

Not wanting to be party to the lowering of her own estimated net worth, he shrugged his shoulders and told her he'd never owned one. She cocked her head to the side, opening her eyes wider. She stretched her arms in his direction, making small circles with her forefingers. It was as if she was leading a symphony called, "Out with it, Chump." Accordingly, he followed.

"As far as American watches go, I've only had Hamiltons, Walthams, and Elgins."

"Okay, but if you are a collectah, you have to know something about them. They're a big company; I think they're still around."

Responding as if he were in a real conversation, he said, "I think someone bought the name, but the original Bulova Company has been out of business or sold awhile back. Which if anything is good for yours, as an original one is rarer."

"Whatya think I could get for it?"

Claiming to be a collector and not having given her a single number to this point, Max went to restoring his credibility.

"Is it gold? Is the dial rectangular or round? Does it run?"

She made him go over each of the questions a few times before answering.

"I'm not really positive at all. I think gold or maybe gold filled, who knows. We didn't have as much back when he bought it, so maybe it wasn't pee-yaw. Fred was not a bad guy, but I was the brains of the operation."

Becoming more irritated, she then admitted the truth by looking down and quietly reprimanding Fred's soul.

"I told you to buy the gold one, yah big dope yah."

Looking back to Max, she continued, "But it's still an antique! It's circular, that I do know. I haven't wound it in faw-evah, so who knows? I don't think it does run. But like I said, I haven't wound it in a long time, so maybe it does. Maybe it ticks and maybe it don't."

After she chuckled at her own last summation, and before she could open the cash register drawer that housed her tongue and clang him for a number, Max pre-empted her with a look and "hmmm," alerting her that an estimate was forthcoming. Using the given plethora of precise particulars she had relayed, he silently figured the watch's value at about sixty dollars. He realized that only doubling that amount for diplomacy's sake might not be diplomatic enough.

"I would guess around one hundred and eighty dollars."

She did not hide her displeasure from this insult. She appeared to try to close her eyes by forcing every muscle on her face except her eyelids. She screeched while gyrating her forefingers at him, as if they were a pair of angry Rattlesnake tails. Having no antidote on his person, he could only interject between her various sound effects.

"That's what a dealer at one of the shows I go to might give for it. That's wholesale or less. To an individual or a retail dealer, a lot more, I'm sure. Way more."

She seemed to regain her breath. Her wrists relaxed, and one slid down into her purse. It came out with a dollar bill, which she waved like a flag.

"Who's gonna get Grandma a Perrier first?"

What he really wanted to express was, *How I would like to jump for that dollar bill and not stop running until swimming in the original source of your requested liquid. I pity the poor bastard that first owned the watch, knowing how he must have been praying for his own mainspring to break and time to end.*

Max, so as not to let gloom win over, also fantasized relaying, *How happy Fred's soul must be, to now be in a position where (god willing) he could hear his watch described with, "I bequeath preceding the description."*

"Thank you, Stephen; your grandmother was completely parched. Boy oh boy you have inflation working for you."

Stephen jumped and snagged the bill from her teasing hand. Max's tiny respite ended in, "I got another clock."

This was spoken over Stephen's little brother's repeated wails of, "It's not fair; he pushed me!"

Max's thoughts, despite fearing the forthcoming round, benevolently moved to how he could quiet the younger brother and help even the score between them. He pictured waving a twenty-dollar bill in front of Stephen, and twenty-one in front of his little brother, all in front of the open window.

"It's a Seth Thomas clock with a folksy picture painted on it. It's called a banjo clock. Do they bring any real money?"

Max had been to the National Association of Watch and Clock collector's largest convention only three months prior. He distinctly remembered speaking with a guy who had a booth full of those same clocks. They ranged in price from four hundred to seven hundred dollars, with two exceptionally rare examples for twelve hundred. Max now had a basis with which to apply higher multiples to keep himself out of harm's way. But rather than math, Max thought of how for the first time she seemed to know exactly what she had. Combining that with his newly acquired battlefield fatigue, he could only shrug his shoulders and weakly repeat, "I really only collect Sessions."

"Well then what would you guess?"

While looking in the other direction he pleaded, "I

couldn't."

Reassuringly she encouraged, "Ahhh go ahead, even just a guess."

"Well it would only be just a guess, and not a real educated one at that. Seeing how it is hand painted, it must be something pretty valuable. I don't know—it's only just a guess."

He spoke the rest more like he was asking a question.

"Maybe three or four thousand dollars."

He braced for the unknown. He had equal trepidation that he might have overdone the snow job, burying him deeper in the process. She was pushing her hands on the arms of the chair with the force of a gymnast during the final dismount off the parallel bars. Whether or not she did three flips and a couple of twists before arriving on her feet, Max could not tell you. He only opened his eyes as she stood above him. She repeatedly raised one hand and then the other skyward, jerking them down to point at him. As each forefinger came in line with his face, she fired, "Yaw wrrong! Yaw wrrong! Yaw wrrong! My cousin spoke to an antiques dealer in Nyack who is an expert and he said they go for six thousand big ones!"

She walked back to her chair, laughing at his stupidity. He tried to laugh along and cowered, "I'd better stick to watches."

"You ought to, bustah."

Max excused himself and went to the bathroom. He ducked the view in the mirror fearing it would induce a torrent of *italic descriptives*, directed this time only at his battered self.

Moments later, Helen arrived. This would not be a news event to the rest of the free world. To Max this godsend was a cross between the cavalry and the senders own son the Baby Jesus. During dinner, the sister did not understand his only joke. Helen thought to help by explaining it to her. Expressionless, big sis grunted, "Okay."

Other than that, with Helen standing guard, dinner was more boring than eventful. Walking home, Helen turned to Max and said, "Tonight counts as one of my treats. Where are you thinking of taking me next time?"

To bed, if I got to deal with this family abuse like I would have to if I were sleeping with you. I might as well.

Max tickled her rib and said, "Wherever you want to go."

WHO'S THE PIMP HERE?

M y formative years as a boxing fan came well after the corruption scandals of the fifties that forced Friday Night Fights off TV, and before the proliferation of cable television in the seventies. As a result of timing, seeing a professional fight on television was a rare treat. It would be preceded by weeks of anticipation.

A decade past this period, shortly after college, I was trying to find work in various aspects of film production. To sustain myself, I found a job minding the door at a nightclub. The hours gave me the free time I needed during the day to search for film work. It also afforded me the time to find distractions to retard that search.

In those days, I considered people that exercised for vanity and fitness alone, and not associated with a particular sport, as narcissists. Joining a gym for Gymrythmics or weightlifting was of no interest, even if I could have afforded a membership.

Passing through the eastern edge of Times Square, at the time a red-light district, I happened on a place called the "Times Square Athletic Club." It was at the top of a long, dark staircase in a dilapidated three-story building. It had a large window facing the street. The window displayed a hand-painted pair of red boxing gloves and the establishment name. Both appeared to have lost unanimous decisions to time and pollution. I climbed up, hoping there might be some well-known fighters to watch spar.

A Puerto Rican guy named Jesse greeted me. His fighting career just over, Jesse was a trainer in training. He had the size and jumpy movements of a flyweight still on the other side of the ropes. Belying his intense stare and rapid New Yorican style of speech were a smile and playful jabs, both pointed at my head within a minute of meeting him. Jesse asked me how old I was and how much I weighed. I said, "Around a hundred and seventy." Before I could tell him my age, he suggested that I should slim down to middleweight. I was flattered that by just looking at me he would consider me a future contender. I told him I was not interested in becoming a fighter. This did not deter his forward momentum. After the third or fourth explanation of my real reason for being there, I joked that my interest was more in watching the gloves bounce off other people's heads.

Immediately (in his own mind) he accommodated my request by lightly bouncing an ungloved hand off the side of my head. He feigned and ducked as he helpfully began pointing out, "If you want to avoid the gloves from bouncing off your fucking head, you got to watch how the other muthafucka moves."

In spite of his misinterpretation of my wisecrack, I was grateful for his suggestion. His "hands on approach" was beginning to raise my interest. He told me "The monthly fee is five dollars a month."

I was soon on my way to buying the suggested gear. Jesse recommended G&S, an old-line New York maker of boxing equipment. He told me that he "used a pair of G&S bag gloves for ten fucking years and the motherfuckas almost look new."

I relayed this testimonial, sans the color, to the guy at G&S sporting goods. He responded straight-faced, almost apologetically. "Yeah, well we've improved them a lot since then."

That character hooked me on the sport before changing into my new training shorts. Surprisingly it took little time to make friends and to realize I was in the minority of members who had not served time in jail. Of the few others who hadn't, I assumed it was in their future. Seven members were fighting actively as professionals. One of them had lost a decision only he disputed in a world title fight.

After a month or so, I met my first pro. He was an eighteen-year-old Irish American fighter who commuted from Long Island. He was undefeated after six professional fights. At the time of our meeting, Glenn was sitting on a bench in the locker room with his head in his hands crying. I have read about fighters becoming dejected for periods after losing a fight they have trained months for and dreamed about for longer. All young fighters take huge, obvious risks in their real or imagined title march. A roadblock via a loss can be devastating. Curiously, I knew this guy had not been beaten yet. I surely would have been made aware if he had just fought. I wondered if there had been a tragedy in his family, or if a member of the opposite sex had succeeded in doing what no man had yet been able to accomplish.

I tried to look away and even started to move my gym stuff as a sign of respect for whatever tragedy had befallen him. He stopped sobbing and sat motionless in the same position. I then felt compelled to take a couple of steps back in his direction and ask, "Are you okay, buddy?"

He told me he would be and thanked me. Maybe the little attention helped, as he got up and started getting into his gym clothes. He then confided in me that his mother had given him a certain amount of money for the train and food and that he had lost it. The common street swindle of pick the ball from under one of three fast-moving cups had been the culprit. The only people who win are the dealers and his accomplices (that he lets win to encourage the suckers to bet). The dealer's expertise is in cupping (hiding) the ball, employed only when the sucker guesses the right cup that the ball is under.

He carried on about what his mother was going to do to him and how stupid he was. I was as convinced to the extent a New Yorker can be that he hadn't invented this drama in a plan to "cup the ball" from me (the real sucker). I lent him ten dollars to get home to Mom. Despite that being a substantial sum for me, in a certain way I was disappointed when three days later he returned my money with heartfelt thanks.

My developing theory during those three days had come true. You don't have to be devoid of human qualities or spend time in jail to punch other people hard.

Admittedly, I had joined expecting to meet people very different from myself. I learned this was not the case. As I met more of the members, I came to realize that these people were not making distinctions between themselves and me. They were decent enough not to scrutinize me and to simply accept me for how I treated them.

I can't recall how and when Roberto and I became friends, but he became my best friend there. He was, as I had come to know him, a warm and caring person. Bobby was half African American and half Puerto Rican. He was twenty-five and was pursuing a dream of fighting in the golden gloves as a junior lightweight. Roberto was married; his wife worked for him in his business. He served as the pimp, and she served as one of three girls working under his direction. His product was sold as a less friction filled variety of sex. His women worked in peepshow houses, where the man is restricted to putting only his quarter in a slot. That action subsequently lifts a wood panel covering a window. Behind the window is a woman or women fondling themselves. Roberto, like an agent negotiating the terms of the agreement, collected a fee. I assumed he was also their business manager, thus determining the amount of his own compensation.

Roberto came in one day and told me of another pimp having convinced his wife to give him some of her pay without Roberto's knowledge. When he found out, I was expecting to hear the details of an impromptu domestic sparring session. Yet he told me, in a sympathetic tone, of how he felt bad for her, as she herself felt so badly about doing the wrong thing. He further sympathized with, "We've all been talked into doing stupid things."

Roberto was not always as nice or as understanding with others. One day we were chasing each other around the ring without gloves, practicing footwork. A professional fighter by the name of Justice Sosa, who was sharing the ring shadow boxing, snapped, "Fighters don't do that."

I was more than willing to heed his expert counsel and stop right there. Roberto countered this advice with, "You ain't my fucking trainer and mind your fucking business."

Ensuing was the requisite face-to-face screaming. Before the style of battle suggested by our immediate environment—which would heavily favor Justice—broke out, Roberto took a moment to calm himself. He raised his eyebrows and asked Justice, in a much quieter, almost polite tone, "Would you like me to go get my gun?"

Justice screamed, "I'll go get mine, too, like you're the only motherfucker that has one."

Roberto did nothing other than lift his eyebrows a little higher, still looking at him in the same questioning tone. What soon became apparent in this pre-fight stare down was that Justice was less prepared to die defending his theory on the merits of practicing ring footwork solo as was Roberto's willingness to risk all supporting his view that tandem footwork training was at least as beneficial.

After workouts, Jesse, Roberto, and I would routinely go to "Tad's flaming Steaks." Tads had a large glass window facing the street so the passerby could be enticed by the sight of the steaks sizzling on the grill. When a cop walked by, both Roberto and Jesse, possessing various outstanding warrants, would be careful not to aid the window steaks in bringing in these particular people. They would turn away and stoop so low they appeared to be ducking haymakers from an octopus, even though we always sat in the back. I remember Jesse mentioning calmly during a Thursday after dinner conversation, "Oh yeah, I forgot to tell you, I cut somebody Monday."

I can't remember why he cut him, as I think Jesse had forgotten also. That mentioning led to a story by Roberto. Some guy in his apartment house came to his door recently when he wasn't there and asked his wife if he could borrow a TV. This guy had been hovering for weeks, and it was clear he had an illicit interest in Roberto's wife. Immediately upon his wife's telling, knowing this "chumps" excuse for stopping by was bogus, Roberto reported, "Me and my buddies paid his ass a visit."

He stopped without further explanation. I asked what they had done to him. Roberto told me, "We fucked him good."

I questioned, "How did you fuck him?"

He stared at me blankly and said, "We fucked him, that's all."

I first conjectured that they had really hurt him badly or worse, and by not elaborating he was protecting me. That assumption really didn't fly, as he had detailed countless stories to Jessie and me that I wish he hadn't. I can't repeat them, but suffice it to say, when my turn for a criminal admission rolled around, I was certain they would not appreciate my more daring crimes like dining and dashing during road trips to Florida with college buddies. I was in the mood for a vengeance tale, so I persisted. "How did you fuck him?"

He replied a little louder, "We fucked him!"

"Okay, but what did you do to fuck him?"

He put his hands on his hips and leaned his head on his shoulder. Tucking his chin in, his eyes scrunched up and he looked at me as if I were stupid. He said quietly, "We fucked him."

Then he shook his head and said, "What, am I speaking Puerto Rican French here?"

Having worked myself up into curiosity frenzy, I asked, "Yeah, yeah, but how. What exactly did you do?"

He made the okay sign with his left hand and repeatedly jabbed his right pointing finger through the O formed by his other hand. "Fucking, fucking, see?"

He then stood up, impersonating Elvis from the waist down, and asked, "Whattya stupid?"

I started to say, "You mean—?"

Then I stopped myself. He saw me stunned, yet probably unaware of the depth or exact cause of my amazement, defended his actions by saying, "Hey, you go to fuck, and you get fucked!"

The two or three times a week when I feel someone deserves complete and total humiliation and degradation, I think back to what a great idea Roberto had, even if I was only capable of imagining using the leg of a table.

Another time we were discussing careers. I mentioned that I was studying to get a real estate license, and I suggested he might try also. He looked at me, then down at the jailhouse tattoos on his hands, and he answered truthfully, disguising it as a question. "Ah, who's going to buy real estate from me?"

I said nothing, as I knew he was probably right. Curiously, with his background and lack of formal education—the operative word being formal—he'd never put me in an uncomfortable position, as I had him. Well maybe once when he inquired if I had any experience in posting bail.

After finishing our steaks, we headed to Forty-second Street and Eighth Avenue, to the "XXX" something or other where two of his girls were working. Bobby had a discrepancy with the manager concerning the percentage of the take owed to the girls. He believed the house was keeping too much. They negotiated back and forth for some time until Bobby screamed, "Who's the pimp here anyway?"

Without giving the manager a chance to respond, he shouted, "I am the pimp here!"

Pounding on his own chest, he repeated, "I'm the pimp here!"

In bed that night, I chuckled to myself about how what he had said sounded. After the laughs, I thought about how I admired Bobby for taking pride in his work. Knowing him as I did, I only wished people would be willing to buy real estate from him.

I CURED SKLERMISCH

P oking through my desk drawer a few months after graduating college, I pulled out my college transcript. Solely for the sake of keeping occupied, I reviewed it. I noticed that of the one hundred and twenty credit hours I had graduated with, cheating of one form or another had procured or had a positive effect on one hundred twelve of those hours. I thought of all the money spent by my father, my grandmother, and myself. I reflected on all the nonsensical things that I did in the time I was supposed to be studying. A sense of disappointment and regret bordering on self-loathing came over me. How could I have cheated in the ridiculous amount of one hundred twelve hours of higher-level education? And not find a way to cheat in the last eight! My record could have been perfect! From my perspective, that feat would be comparable to a 4.0 average.

Throughout my school career, I never sought the friendship of any teacher. The various abuses of their power and the almost absolute authority took their toll. To reinforce my outlook and take the fun out of whatever text book learning was to be offered at my college, enter English literature 101. The idea of being tested on a book, the reading and comprehension of which can be so personal and individual, offended me from the start. I had to remind myself of the following: They invited me here to take my money, not to redesign their curriculum.

The greasy-gray-haired, khaki clad, pipe-puffing cliché standing in front of me was little more interesting than he was original in dress. Only his loud coughing and equally noisy speech kept the class sleep-free. His raspy voice grew louder after every hack, as if to immediately challenge the results of his self-induced disease. His persona kept him yapping about his take on the book rather than asking anyone else's, or worse prying into my opinion on his subject. Still, it was sometimes interesting to view his proud yet coy smile as he relayed the true meaning of the book. His gospel-like confidence reverberated, as if he had gathered his facts by attending a séance of the dead author the night before class.

After listening to the professor, I was convinced the author's real intent in writing the book was to give my teacher satisfaction and an income by allowing him to reward us with all the real meanings firsthand.

Midway through the semester walking out of his class, a sixty-year-old tweed-coated arm dropped on my shoulder. I looked around at him and moved my head away at the same time. He asked, "How do you like my class?"

I told him, "Fine."

He then covered me in small talk, indicating he was now taking a personal approach. Over the next couple of months, I became friendly with him principally because he extended his and I saw no reason not to. I also like the smell of cherry pipe tobacco.

With two weeks to go in the semester, my self-appointed

mentor offered the class the chance to rewrite their papers. I did so, raising my three papers' average from a C+ to an A-. The other half of what my final grade would be judged on was my test average. Including the final exam, the tests averaged a B. My final grade came in the mail, C+. I went to speak with my friend the professor concerning his shortcomings in basic statistics. He opened the would-be conversation and stymied my ability to communicate with a disclaimer: "But just because we are friends."

My disgust left me unable to offer rational argument on a matter of fifth grade math. I walked out, muttering to myself, "The next time I need a second opinion on my work, I'll reread it!"

After it was too late for this class, I learned one could contest a grade with a third party called an "ombudsmen." I took advantage of that new addition to my vocabulary with a class a few years later. As luck and the collegiate gods would have it, the old literature professor was appointed the ombudsman! He prefaced and almost simultaneously ended our discussion with, "I know Professor Hackbee well, and he is a good Christian."

I replied, "I don't care what Mr. Hackbee does in his spare time. I am only interested in my grade and how it got the way it did, on a non-spiritual level."

The meeting ended with the only things raised being blood pressure and my desire to be done with that place. This abbreviated sit-down reminded me of what I already knew. The college stint wasn't really me. The only way I could win was to climb a makeshift stage, shake some stranger's hand, and pluck my diploma out of his free one.

Four years after graduating, a few friends were having dinner in New York at the behest of the university. My "Early Civilization" history professor and newly appointed fundraiser was the host. By statistical anomaly, I liked this teacher enough to subject myself to this type of sales pitch. In spite of barely passing his course, I liked him because of one particular incident: His classroom dated from 1902. It was thirty feet deep, built on six graduated levels of wood ground down with three-quarters of a century of dirt. The top tier was no more than ten feet higher than the lowest.

Arriving to his class early, a buddy and I discovered a secret hatch leading underneath the floor. We pried open a latch that squeaked and tugged back against us as if protecting King Tut's tomb. We climbed under and forward to where we would be almost directly underneath the teacher. We discussed our plan waiting for the class and our tour guide to Mesopotamia to arrive.

Every time he would launch into some historical fact, we would counter with commentary such as, "That's a lot of bull. How the hell do you know, were you there? Ah shaddup, you bore me!"

Each subterranean outburst would be followed by a tense silence. Next came his probes and somewhat good-natured threats to whoever was behind them. When he and the class discovered what was going on and who was behind it, he had everyone search for a passage door. As soon as that was successfully accomplished, he and an equally heavyset volunteer ran and stood over it. In a few more minutes, we heard sharp metal against metal banging. I assume he took as much demonic pleasure in driving the nails into the sides of the hatch as we had in disrupting his class. He said through the floor, "If you shut up and pay attention I won't mark you absent."

We crawled and maneuvered through three-quarters of a century's worth of filth and debris on our archeological dig to the vent-grate we found some twenty minutes after the hour-long class ended.

My history teacher/scholastic panhandler dominated the

dinner conversation. His mouth stayed in perpetual motion. Between bites of food, he would tell us how successful and how many trillions our non-present classmates had given. Sometimes he would chew and tell at the same time. He subtly moved to asking us all individually how we were doing. My con radar was down, and I did not pick up his manipulations until a few days later. I wish I would have told him, "I would love to give, but every time I go for a job and mention where I graduated, they either throw or laugh me out of the office or trailer."

The final insult and erasure of my real purpose in coming was they did not even pick up the tab.

Fifteen years after this dinner, some nitwit classmate gave the school my caller-unidentified telephone number. Since that time, every six months an underclassman will call begging for funds for my Alma Mata. Once I pledged five thousand just for the fun of listening to various officials plead and beg for the money that they claimed I owed. "Pledged" being the operative word as opposed to gave. On another occasion, an overtly enthusiastic coed asked, "Do you have anything you might like to have printed in the Alumni magazine?"

I told her, "I am an assistant manager trainee at the local McDonalds franchise." After reading that in the next magazine, I assume people that knew me must have thought, "Well, he always acted stupid; I guess he really was."

Six months later, during another telephone mooching session, I asked, "Don't you want to know about me for the Alumni news?"

Before he finished the K in okay, I proceeded to let him know: "Mitchell Belacone is a professional bowler on the PBA tour; his average is 212. He is sponsored by Brunswick & Power Grips. He placed third in the Las

Vegas Open and has had three television appearances on ESPN."

I have a rheumatologist friend from Florence, Italy. Marco spends half his time with his practice in Italy. He spends the other half traveling the world, coordinating various hospitals research into finding a cure for sklermaderma. It is a rare degenerative, painful, and terminal nerve disease. Shortly after his stay with me in New York—with the name of that disease and the telephone ringing in my ear simultaneously—Alfred U. begs again. I state my conditions for donating into a speakerphone. "You print my latest, then I will give you however much you ask for."

He agrees, prompting me to dictate the words he needs to have published to fulfill his consideration for this oral agreement: "Mitchell Belacone is a research chemist working in a private laboratory. He and his partner are currently negotiating with a major pharmaceutical company for distribution of a vaccine they have developed and patented for the treatment of Sklerm—" (Before I could blunder and possibly mislead and hurt innocent people, I defy my educational background and finish the statement with) "Sklermisch."

This latter disease exists only in my imagination. I am sure of this because to date, even after being made aware, no alumnus has called to be treated for his or her Sklermisch.

Another year goes by before they call. I had nothing scripted so I told them I was busy but instructed this latest soon to be dupe to buzz back in an hour, "I am most interested in giving!"

I had forgotten I had been invited to watch Sunday night football at an apartment six floors directly above mine. I brought my handheld telephone for two reasons. First to see if it would work within the claimed half-mile from the base set. Secondly, I had no intention of letting this school make me miss a down of the game. I hardly settled in upstairs when someone asked me why I'd brought my phone. I told her and incidentally the ten others within earshot, "I am expecting an important business call."

My phone rang at the beginning of a commercial. Within seconds, I had the student on the other end taking my dictation. *"Mitchell Belacone is the third member of his immediate family to be accepted into the French Foreign Legion as an officer. He has been appointed a post as a munitions specialist and will be leaving for his tour in March."*

The fact that the French Foreign legion had disbanded ten years earlier proved lost on the editorial staff of the alumni paper, although not on my new friends in the room. When asked for an explanation, I gave them a highly abridged version of what you have read here, highlighting the previous posts in the school paper. Other than the television and the tail end of a few audible smirks, all became quiet as the game returned. A few moments later, my friend and host's wife blurts out, "My mother has Sklermaderma."

I immediately retraced my words, hoping I had not been too light or comical in that part of the retelling. The heads in the room went silently back and forth between the two of us as if we were battling out the final set at Wimbledon. Seeing the opportunity to help a friend and distance myself from any insult that might have been taken, I said, "My friend Marco the doctor will be in town in two weeks; I am sure he would be happy to see your mother if she wanted. He heads the world organization. At the very least she would hear about the latest research, directly from the source."

She thanked me and said she would ask her. The next

day she called to give me the okay to set up the appointment.

The airport exit sign came into view, signaling the start of a two-day race for Marco to make it to all his meetings. He was to see my friend's mother that first evening. After coming home late that night, I greeted him with a "Well?"

He told me, "I called her first as agreed and she canceled."

He looked at my face now shaped like a question mark and continued speaking. "Due to the disfiguring nature of this disease, people with it often go into a shell avoiding others. They give up hope."

Although increasing my sympathy for her, this eased some of my guilt for being party to the wasting of his precious time in New York. The following morning my upstairs friend came by and had no explanation for his mother-in-law's cancellation. Bobby and I had been friends for only a few months. Thus, I was even more wary about sticking my beak into matters so personal and delicate as a family member's medical situation. His tone or expressions did not hint at the wasted opportunity that I was feeling. We talked a little about the game two nights earlier before he got up to leave. As he walked out of my door, I barked at him as if he were hard of hearing, "Hey, make this happen!"

He said nothing in return, stutter stepped, then kept walking. I slunk back inside contemplating what I had just done. I wondered what kind of jerk tries to take charge of a neighbor's relative's medical situation three months after meeting him. Wondering ceased quickly, as there was a clear answer. I am exactly that type of jerk!

With the aid of high quantities of schmoozalube by Marco to his schedule, he wedged her in for a meeting that night. I spent the whole day hoping someone would be the better for all this but would have happily settled for no one being the worse.

Until she had called me that night after Marco's visit, I had never met or spoken to Bobby's mother-in-law. I picked up my phone and was having difficulty trying to make out anything of what she was screaming. She was at a level of mania with which I was unfamiliar. It took me a few minutes to decipher that Marco had already left. I was feeling a lot of not so happy things, including but not limited to queasy. What made me get involved? I had no knowledge of Marco's bedside manner. Head of the world organization of Skleraderma? For all I knew their membership counted no more members than the one for Sklermisch! So much for my good standing in the building and what was left of this poor lady's sanity. Had he used his expert knowledge to inform her of how many months she had left? Had he just been arrogantly matter of fact in the reiteration of the grim prognosis? Whatever he had told her, it was a clear fact that he had touched, then punched and stomped, the bull's-eye of her central nervous system.

I finally summoned up the volume and courage to try to get her to tell me what he had told her. Out of a series of vocal gyrations and histrionics that would be foreign even to the ears of a game show host came a, "You no more have Skleraderma than I do."

My ear drums were taxed another half a minute before I could get her to clarify that he had told her with no uncertainty that she did not have Skleraderma.

It had been seven years since her high-priced Park Avenue rheumatologist had handed down his version of a death sentence. He deduced his prognosis on two facts: First, she tested positive for the disease. The test at the time it was taken had a one in four error ratio. Secondly, she had dried blotches of skin that were similar to those of

Sklermaderma patients. Hers were probably a reaction to a prescribed drug. She never consulted with another doctor because she believed she already had the best, and there was no cure or effective treatments anyway.

In lieu of cigars that I don't smoke, I sat back and settled for a deep breath of air. I heard bagpipes and drum rolls as I figured the only thing between me, and my just reward was the where and when. No, the thought of having helped someone in need is not enough! In reflection, I pieced together the twenty-year string of lunafied, disparate, and seemingly senseless events and circumstances that all melded together in order to lead her back off her perceived ledge to doom. God and Knoodnicks work in mysterious ways.

I finally did get my Congressional Medal of Honor in the form of a free meal at the "cured" patient's Christmas party. I owed my college a debt of gratitude for helping me in whatever roundabout way to rid the world of disease. Maybe that's worth another five-thousand-dollar pledge. Then again, maybe not, as this is in writing.

All is well with my standing in the building, although that is less of a concern now. I am headed to Bolivia to assume the ambassadorship. I hereby pass on an invitation to all of you. If you are down that way, feel free to drop by the embassy and say hello. Tell the guards I said "no appointmento necessario." While you are there, maybe you will meet some of my classmates, all of whom were previously invited via the alumni news.

THE YOGA CLASS RAPIST

The Day-Care Center Pedophiles Preface

Brad sat in front of his television, fists balled, wishing he could bounce them off the man of the couple on the screen . . . if there would be no legal recourse, just a moral decision. He fantasized that he could exact justice with a couple of tugs on the trigger of his stainless steel .357 magnum. Under the right circumstances, Brad knew that he could take another person's life. Two years earlier when he was twenty-four, he had tried to do exactly that to a boy of sixteen who stood between Brad and what Brad had to do. When thinking of that moment, more than anything else, he felt a sense of pride. If the situation called for it, he could do what needed to be done.

I'd dissect them like a pair of high school frogs. How could anybody be that fucking sick? Those satanic motherfuckers probably gave reassuring smiles to the parents when they dropped their kids off. If the devil stuck me in the ass with his pitchfork, it wouldn't make me believe he exists any more than those two twisted animals doing what they did.

As he watched the rest of the news, his mind stayed on the couple. He imagined the various ways that he would torture them before executing them. Almost all the children under the couple's supervision had affirmed that they had been either inappropriately touched or penetrated.

Children are known to be more honest than adults. What's the point of a trial? So that some idiot juror can pronounce them innocent in order to get home to her soap opera? So that some money-grubbing lawyer can dupe a jury into letting them skate free? Kill them; pedophiles can't be cured.

Throughout the coming years, Brad's memory revisited that newscast. Each time it did, his solace was taken, knowing that, when in prison, those types of degenerates are tossed into the lower rungs of hell.

Fuck 'em, I hope they suffer each and every day in there.

Shafting the Shafters

Brad's father, a real estate salesman for the last ten years, had done business and was friendly with two brothers who owned a construction company. In that tenth year, both brothers proposed to Brad Sr. that they go into the real estate development business together. A partnership was formed. The brothers handled the construction side and Brad Sr. handled the business end. After achieving moderate success in a few different fields, Brad's father had found his niche late in life as a commercial real estate developer.

Every three years thereafter, Brad Sr. would go to the Mercede dealership to pay cash for three new identical—save for his partners' color choices—company sedans. One year at the dealership, Brad Sr. overheard a customer crying to the sales manager.

"My wife says I can't keep this car, I gotta return it and get a four-door car. She says 'that thing is nothing but a P-wagon and you ain't keepin' it!'"

As the man was a longtime customer, the dealership acquiesced. To be clear, P is not an abbreviation for station. Bingo! As that customer left, Brad's dad, a widower of many years, swooped in and cut a deal on an almost virgin ivory 1982 380 SL two-door P-wagon. So excited with his new prop, he barely remembered to buy the anthracite gray metallic and orient red four-door sedans for his partners. The motivation behind his personal choice, as wise and admirable as it seemed to him, didn't work out in practice. At sixty-six years old, Brad Sr. found this low-to-the-ground sports car too difficult to get in and out of.

At a Greek diner in New Jersey, Brad Sr.'s stance on not helping his son financially changed with one scratch of his pen: He signed over the title. Brad as an in-shape and good-looking thirty-year-old was in a better position to utilize this car for its intended purpose. As an afterthought, Brad felt relieved to now own reliable transportation. He drove it from New York back to his adopted hometown of Houston.

. . . Oh please! If not for the peacock effect of these sorts of cars, they would cease to exist, and most guys would take the bus . . .

The first day back at the YMCA, between games of basketball, three different acquaintances, at separate moments, questioned him about what he'd paid for the car. No foreplay, they just flat out asked. He wondered; *did they see me park? How did the word spread so quickly? Why is this everybody's business?*

He gave each guy a different number.

"You must have a big lien on that car?"

Prudence limited him to only think what he wanted to say: *The only thing that leans on that car is me, when I'm tired.*

143

Unfortunately, it took more than that one afternoon for Brad to learn, the world revolves less around the green you can count and more around that color as seen on people's faces. With the sale of his other car, Brad now had a little cash freed up to search for a small sailboat. A captive audience of one female, or two if fantasy played itself out, on Galveston Bay was the impetus behind the planned expenditure.

. . . It might appear that Brad was hereditarily predisposed to this kind of plotting. But consider: Be it jewelry or even just a drink, it's common for healthy males with a few extra dollars in their pocket to set purchased romantic traps . . . (I warned you in the disclaimer.)

An encounter with the shifty antics of a local boat broker, which coincided with Brad's largest real estate sale, led him to let that salesman flounder. He upped the ante and shopped elsewhere for a live-aboard sailboat. The two largest obstacles he had to overcome were, one, he knew a fraction more than nothing about sailboats or sailing, and, two, if he did buy a decent boat of that size, he would be broke again.

Locating a sailboat in Newport, Rhode Island, Brad and a buddy drove the land prop up east to get a deal done on a floating one. The target was a 1975 Lord Nelson 41' named *Black Hawk*. It had the look and lines of a classic yacht from the '30s but with a Fiberglas hull. She had enough teak above and below to put her own personal dent in the Myanmar rain forest. The contract price was $48,000. The surveyor warned, "It will take at least $20,000 just to make it safe to sail. Add another $20,000 to bring justice her to her cosmetically."

The seller was the famous, single-handed around-the-world racer Mark Parson. Mark was considered a local hero. As the story goes, during one of his two solo circumnavigation races, Mark was helped by a small power boat to keep him off the rocks during a storm on a faraway coast. The people on that boat said they would never utter a word, and no one would ever be the wiser.

Mark replied, "I would know."

He radioed in what happened and was disqualified.

Proving that Brad's expenditure was motivated by a search for adventure beyond bouncing around in the water and becoming yet another hue of green called "seasick," Brad was announcing to every woman he met in the sailing circles of Newport that he would be looking for crew to get it back to Galveston Bay. Brad and his buddy drove back to Houston while the title documentation was being completed. The plan was to fly back after that was done, close the deal, oversee a few months of work, and then find a crew to sail it back to Galveston Bay.

He thought the name *Black Hawk* too sinister and was ready to change it. The broker warned him that changing a boat's name is bad luck. He heeded the broker's advice. To quote the self-admitted woman-beater John Lennon, life is what happens to you while you are busy making other plans. In Brad's case, specifically, Mother Nature is what happened to him while he was busy making other plans, with 1985's Hurricane Gloria giving a beating to his barely floating industrialized sized chick magnet to be. The broker mailed him pictures of the victimized yacht. Knowing as little as Brad did about boats, he was ready to run from this deal the minute "Honest Mark" would try to encourage him to still go through with the purchase. Brad's calls to Mark weren't answered or returned. That non-act spurred a curiosity. The broker knew nothing as well and recommended a lawyer. "Space Shot," as he was called around the courthouse, couldn't find out anything either. Brad's title transfer agent got wind that a sale to another party was about to go down. That transaction would result in the loss of her fee. She alerted Brad, who in turn phoned Space Shot.

Mark Parson was one of the most famous and connected people in the Newport yachting world. He found a marine surveyor who put the damages at an exorbitantly high $38,000. Mark and Brad's contract called for the insurance money to be turned over to the buyer. Mark's plans did not coincide with that contract. His idea was to pocket the insurance proceeds and sell *Black Hawk* to his new buyer. The new buyer had lost to Brad on his original bid six weeks back. He accepted 20 percent off his original offer price. He was aware that almost all of what was damaged during the hurricane needed to be repaired or replaced even before the storm. Understandably, Mark looked at Hurricane Gloria as heaven-sent.

As Brad was arriving to court, Mark shouted from the top of the courthouse steps, "You're playing a dangerous game. You're in way over your head."

Brad, feigning an overly sympathetic tone—*too bad for me, huh?* —"Hey, asshole, I been to jail before. It ain't nothin' new for me! You're in my town, motherfucker, and I'm gonna fuck your ass, bitch!"

Marky, Marky, I'm flattered, but before it comes to that, maybe you ought to rethink this solo sailing thing.

The exchange served only to encourage Brad that the money for the lawyer was well spent. There was something to be gained here. On three different occasions, after Parson and his lawyer pleaded their parts, the judge screamed at them, "Yeah OK, but who tried to cheat who?"

The zigzag course plotted by Parson pushed Brad's time frame into late fall in Newport. Consequently, Brad trucked his boat back to Texas after receiving a $38,000 Judge

Israel–ordered discount. In essence, he bought the boat for $10,000 plus legal fees.

Working alongside the craftsmen gave Brad invaluable lessons into the construction and mechanics of the boat. His personal experience with the workers was positive, save one redneck owner of a machine shop. Every meeting with Hal came with at least one insultingly lowball offer for his Benz, which he had to repeatedly remind him was not for sale. Hal talked neophyte Brad into to keeping a propeller shaft that should have been rejected for its damaged threading. He almost duped Brad into having his son perform $5,000 of unnecessary surgery on the electrical system.

The foreman of the yard where the work was being done told Brad, "If Hal won't replace the shaft, go to Nguyen Machine Works. They do all the work on the shrimp boats."

Although he trusted the foreman more than Hal, he was still hesitant because of all the slandering Hal had dished out on his fiercest competitors, the "know-nothing Viet Cong gooks."

Brad, having never spoken with a Vietnamese person didn't know what to expect. This was the mid-1980s, and the war-era propaganda was still deeply ingrained in him. He was clearly prejudiced as to their level of civilization. As a country we had not yet come to the realization and admission that, in many regards, they are better than us.

Nguyen's English was almost fluent, and his degree of courtesy even higher. He delivered a perfectly threaded prop shaft 46 percent cheaper than Hal's defective version. So taken aback and pleased by this was Brad that he invited Nguyen and his brother to lunch. Both were lighthearted and entertaining. As the three watched some seedy locals come in, one of the brothers shrugged his shoulders while adopting a facial expression suggesting that this was not the first time that he proposed, "The only way to avoid this trash is to reopen in Palm Beach."

The younger brother had errands to run after lunch, so Brad offered to drive Nguyen back to their shop. In the distance, Brad saw two guys chatting in the parking lot of Hal's Machine Works. He prayed one was Hal.

Brad pulled the car over. "Hey, Nguyen, do you want try driving this?"

"Sure, thanks."

"Just until you reach the light, can you please drive real slowly?"

As Brad fully reclined his passenger seat, the bemused Nguyen, after approaching Hal's shop, suddenly couldn't hold back his laughter. Brad reached over with his left hand and flashed the halogen high beams. According to Nguyen, the whites of Hal's eyes flashed back even brighter. That night Brad answered the phone to hear this decibel-rich tune.

"Why was the gook driving your car?"

"It was a test drive, he dug it, and I'm seriously thinking of selling it to him."

"Well, fuck you, I offered to buy it first!"

"Sorry, Hal, as much as I like you, he offered $5,400 more than you."

Brad's New World

Work was completed; most agreed that *Black Hawk* was the most beautiful yacht at the marina. Within a week, Brad walked into a modeling agency with pictures of his sailboat, offering it for photo shoots. In less than a minute, the thirty-seven-year-old female manager saw through Brad's proposal. No matter, she was more than happy to serve as his booking-agent-in-reverse. Under just one condition: Each time she stocked the cargo hold, she and her boyfriend were on the crew list. Over the following year, a few of the most beautiful women of Houston paralleled the waist-high anatomically correct V berth. Brad dreamed of a soulmate. His aim wasn't to sleep with as many women as he had. Although in doing so, he felt some sense of accomplishment and a satisfactory or, better said, satisfying return on his investment.

. . . OK, I hear ya, but in the mid '80s, he wasn't planning on telling this story on a modern-day talk show.

He was looking for his true love, albeit at a faster pace and with less patience than the average guy. Brad also learned to enjoy sailing.

The recently vibrant Houston economy was now dead in the water. Two years after *Black Hawk* limped into Houston on a gurney; it set sail for Charleston, South Carolina. The new town had easier access to the Atlantic and, as he was soon to learn, the coed-centric College of Charleston. Even eight days at sea can greatly exaggerate one's need for human companionship. At a pub on his third night in town, he met a guy and two girls who appeared to be near his age. As touring other people's boats was one of his favorite pastimes, he assumed the same was true for others. He invited them back to his boat for beers. Walking back from the marina store with another six-pack, he overheard them chatting below.

Female guest 1: "I could never live in something so small."

Female guest 2: "It moves around too much for me."

Male guest: "It would be like living in a basement."

Typically, marine insurance does not cover the sinking of a heart. After popping the top on her can, wearing a coy smile, Guest 1 asked, "Do you take it out much?"

"Hardly ever, it needs a new engine."

College girls have more time on their biological clocks and thus were usually far less demanding as to his level of commitment. They often viewed him as an adventure and wrote off the encounter to practice. After the act or acts, they were usually as relieved to rid themselves of him as the other way around. Walks through the College of Charleston campus yielded a seemingly endless supply of free passes. He felt this necessary to satisfy his urges while on the hunt for a more serious mate. More than any other manufactured item for consumption, Charleston is known to be the world's leading producer of gossip. At first, he was entertained by the nonsensical blabber about him that wafted back his way. As a few years went by, he began to learn its destructive powers. He was slowly becoming aware that if he slept with too many more women, there would be no more women. Worse, one mini abandonment after another, he was better understanding of the harm these trysts could cause. At the end of each union, even those initiated by the women, he felt he was further surpassing his lifetime quota for hurting them. He began to keep his largest prop off center stage on early dates. He was hoping to a find a more honest emotional connection.

One date that didn't match that description was named Emily. After dinner, they went back to her new apartment. They were sitting on the floor as she had yet to purchase a sofa. If not interesting enough to be a keeper, Emily was at least bubbly and playful. After telling her a story of how he recently sold an airline on a bogus story to cancel his reservation without charge. Prompted, she told one along similar lines.

"My sister got out of a year-long membership at her gym after three months without paying a dime."

"How did she manage that one?"

You know that look when you tell someone a story of how you did something bad or sneaky and got away with it. Your shoulders hunched together, a closed-mouth smile, your head and jaw jutted out? She didn't affect anything like that. The only thing Brad could sense was an immense sisterly pride.

"She told the manager that a trainer was sexually harassing her."

"Was the guy?"

"No, but it worked."

He considered that she might have used her sister as an alter ego for this retelling so that she could speak it with only the glee she felt. Coming from this seemingly sweet young thing, it appeared out of character. No enjoyment taken in hearing it; he now knew to avoid physical contact. The evening ended pleasantly and soon after her admission. At home, he considered making a second date to try to get this confession on tape. That poor bastard needed his name cleared. He quickly thought of the dangers of getting involved in a stranger's business of this nature. *Obviously, she has no boundaries. If she spots the recorder, what will stop her from pinning something similar on me?* He thought it best to just walk away. The fact that he did, haunted him more as time went by.

A local orthopedist buddy told him about an ex-actress patient of his, Mandy. She had just moved back from Los Angeles and was pushing the doctor to get fixed up with "the guy who drives around in the little Corvette convertible, do you know him?"

After passing this info along to Brad, the doctor continued, "Listen, I told her you weren't much on commitments."

Brad understood the doctor's need to protect himself

151

and his patient with that disclaimer. In fact, he was thankful for it. Still, he was hesitant, as fixups can backfire on the fixer-upper. While not a fan of skinny, from a medium-long shot away, he could see that her acting career skidded off the rails and into a McDonald's. She was close to his age, and as he felt no physical attraction, the dinner date was a matter of passing the time as pleasantly as possible before paying the check. When he dropped her off, she asked, "Would you like to come in for a glass of wine?"

Not wanting to hurt her feelings with a flat-out rejection, he accepted. One glass later, Mandy disappeared. She returned, wearing something more comfortable for her— and uncomfortable for him. She snuggled close and moved in for a kiss. He normally liked women who removed guessing from the equation. As he saw no possibility of a continuation, he feared the risk of damaging his friendship with the doctor. After the kiss, he smiled and hoped the one would suffice. He said nothing to convey his feelings, as he hated condescending pregame, or no-game, speeches when given to him. That thoughtfulness helped none; she pounced. Rushed and confused, with his motor not in full go mode, he tried his best, which turned out to be near his worst. Oftentimes, as a preplanned exit strategy he would intentionally underperform. This was not the case here, as there was almost nothing to hold back. With a few gymnastically notable exceptions, he did not judge intercourse by his partner's technical skills. It was all about the quality of emotions, the connection produced. Being that there weren't any positive ones to be considered here, Brad never called her again, and she never called him. Thankfully, he received no blowback from the doctor when he saw him next.

A Storm in the Port

Brad had a pushy and kooky real estate agent friend named Betty. He was one of a few that found her entertaining, mostly because he enjoyed watching her cut loose on the public at large. In her special case, he felt the need to make it clear from the beginning that he was only interested in a friendship. She often hinted at more but settled for being invited out on the boat from time to time. Knowing his audience, with trepidation he relayed a story to her attributed to Groucho Marx.

"Groucho spotted an attractive woman seated alone at a table in a restaurant. He walked over and very graciously asked, 'Pardon me miss, are you eating alone this evening?'

"A little taken aback, yet welcoming of his advance, she answered, 'Well, yes, I am?'

" 'Why, what's wrong with you?' "

Most men won't hit women for any reason. Not necessarily the case with other men. But even though Betty mostly used this borrowed Grouchoism as a ballsy pickup line, when she preformed her version of it, Brad made sure to watch at a safe distance from the unsuspecting dupe. Her overuse of the put-down left him regretting having fed it to her.

On one evening's downtown outing, Betty brought along a friend. Rochelle was good-looking enough and the type that turns their hands loose on you, seemingly to accentuate points in the conversation. He couldn't distinguish if she was just the touchy-feely type, making her intentions known, or just liked making sport of men.

"Betty told me, you have a beautiful boat."

With Betty in range, "What does she know?"

Betty's incessant need of attention, and her competitiveness with both Brad and Rochelle, had her happy to enter into the fray. "More than you think I know."

"Oh? And about what, exactly, do you know so much?"

With a huge smile that made the subject of her answer obvious, "Oh, about a lot of things."

"And how did you become so educated in this public domain?"

"I've got friends."

"So do I," Brad said, stretching his neck to get his head closer to Betty for only the first two words of his reply, ". . . I think, but that doesn't mean I know everything about you."

"And whose fault is that?"

With a smile that signaled he wasn't going there, "So Rochelle, Betty told me you enjoy knitting."

After an hour of more good-natured banter between the three, Betty announced that she had an early appointment in the morning. When Betty was in the ladies' room and with the confidence gained from Rochelle's fingerprints covering the top half his shirt, Brad asked, "Would you be interested in a nightcap on the boat? I'll drive you back whenever you like."

She smiled her consent. The touch to his waist was clearly more than to emphasize a point. During the drive, "Do you live far from the boat?"

"About a half mile."

He had a good idea where she was going with her question. Rather than let her question dangle, he followed up his answer with, "Why?"

"Then let's just go there."

They carried the first glass of wine into the bedroom. It quickly progressed into as sexual as can be with clothes on. Ten minutes later, still fully clothed, she blurted out, "Stop!"

"Are you OK? I'm sorry; I thought you were into it."

After three or four seconds of silence, she smiled and tried to resume the bedroom chatter.

Confused and still scared that he might have been too forceful, "I'm sorry if I was too pushy, are you OK, Rochelle, really?"

After another scripted pause, "I'm fine . . ."

In Charleston and Houston, too often for his taste, clothed wrestling matches were a part of the process. They made him wait for it—or, so to speak, fight for it. The game was not to his liking. He thought, *why put me through this, to irritate me? If you want it harder, just tell me. I don't see this in the movies; where do they learn this? It's just going into your negative column for using your built-in advantage to put me in pain and manipulate me into having to think up more lies than I would normally need to.*

That's one style of priming his engine not to his liking. Others would be the following two examples: The first was with a girl from his friend's Houston modeling agency. About three-quarters of the way through the lovemaking, she asked, "Are you gay?"

Whaaat? . . . No, why would you ask me something like that now?

"Because you fuck like a fifteen-year-old boy."

After sticking her tongue out at his newly warped face, she spit on him. Rather than wipe it off his face and ask for an explanation of how a guy in his late twenties should fuck, instincts took over. He flipped her over, grabbed her hair, and did the same thing he was doing before, except much rougher. When he finished, it was as if he snapped out of a trance. Struck with terror for his level of aggression, fearing that he might have hurt her, he dismounted. He was wary of touching her to turn her over to see her face. Still kneeling, he leaned to her side to see her expression. She had a most peaceful and satisfied smile; she mimed him a kiss.

The second was also a first date in Houston. While they were having sex in his apartment, she pulled away and jumped out of bed. She kept both heart rates up by running around laughing, while grabbing his breakable possessions to smash on the floor. Similar results as the first incident. Both encounters scared and angered him enough to make him swear he would never let himself be used in such a potentially dangerous way again.

"Rochelle, do you want to finish the wine downstairs?"

"I'm comfortable here."

Her seductive tone, coupled with her hands grazing the top of his pants, still did not influence him to resume physical contact.

While squeezing his face, she said, "What's the matter, afraid to take what you want?"

On cue, the friction returned to pre- "stop" levels. Within fifteen seconds, she blurted out a loud, "Stop it now!"

"What's the matter? I'm so sorry, are you OK?"

"I'm fine."

"Are you sure?"

She had transformed the haven of his bedroom into a creepy place. Whether it was her game, or she was just nuts, he wanted her gone.

She playfully poked at him, which made her seem even freakier and scarier.

"Maybe we ought to try this another night; honestly, I'm feeling a little funny about all of this."

As they were driving past the marina on the way back into town, in the sweetest and saddest voice she could manufacture, "I thought you were going to show me your boat."

"Let's do it another night. I don't think tonight is our night."

As they were close to her apartment just off Broad Street, "Is here good?"

She nodded yes. He pulled the car over; she got out and stood slightly off to the side of it, without moving. She appeared to be lost, not ready to cry, rather frozen in a daze. He had never inappropriately touched a woman or tried to coerce one with anything more nefarious than charm. As this was before he'd had any Latin girlfriends, he had never even yelled back at one. Even with his dogs, who needed him to be their master, he always had tried to figure out what they wanted to do first. Yet he imagined this is how a woman might behave after a sexual assault. He was torn between getting out of his car to comfort her and getting away. The pull to help was strong, yet he remained in his seat. He only watched until she walked to her door and let herself in. Thinking himself spineless, guilt began to meld with his enormous fear. He wished he had taken it slower.

Driving home, the following thoughts came almost as revelations, accompanied by a sigh of relief.

Thank God we kept our clothes on, let alone do it. What in the fuck was that all about?

Still plenty shook up, early the next day he called Betty and recounted a filtered version to protect Rochelle's privacy. Betty responded.

"Her sister told me she likes to fight."

That took most of the pressure off. He was likely not alone in his experience. There were other people who could back him up, should it come to that. Brad's feelings were moving from fear to disgust until he concluded that this was just her sick shtick.

A lot of women need drama. This one needed an opera, and I was cast as an extra. He waited for months to duck the gossip boomerang he felt sure was coming for his neck, but it didn't. His thoughts of her were mostly sympathetic.

A Bumpy Voyage

One year later, on a warm, early-spring Saturday he invited three Lebanese doctor friends for a sail. Two guys and a woman named Abdel. They brought hummus, tabouli, and a twenty-six-year-old intern named Melisa. She in turn invited her best friend, Julie. As they were not shark fishing and in need of chum, Brad wondered why anyone would drag Julie and her sour personality along. Neither woman was hooked romantically with any of the doctors. Still, as they came with them, he kept his distance. Call it courtesy from one form of professional to another. Hence, he made conversation with his seductive talents almost fully furled. Melisa was a petite blonde from upstate Georgia newly moved to Charleston. She had shoulder-length Nordic, see-through blond hair, smooth skin; overall, more cute than gorgeous. On the way back into the harbor while passing Fort Sumter, powered by her second cocktail, the Southerner fired off her first canon shots in the Yankee's direction. She snuggled up next to him at the helm station. Caught off guard by the unexpected move, he slid half a foot to his right.

"Would you like to try steering her?"

"Why do you call your boat a she?"

"All boats are referred to in the feminine."

"This one shouldn't be."

"Why, because it's named after a male Indian?"

"Take a look at the very front of your boat."

Black Hawk had a 3½-foot bowsprit jutting out from the

bow at a 120-degree angle.

With raised eyebrows and a studying smirk that intentionally showed he was hiding more, "I see your point."

As she seemed so fine, the analogy had him believing she must be woozy from the sun and her drink. He didn't want to jump into the huge opening left to him. The potential embarrassment that only he believed she might feel later led him to trail off only with a muttered, "More man than me."

Still ignoring his offer to steer the boat, she grabbed his front pocket and pulled him toward her. As a captain, you have to make sure that nobody is putting themselves in danger. *Not that kind of danger!*

. . . Sailing is often riskier than it is portrayed to be. During the little voyage, Abdel had perched herself on top of the wooden rail in the stern. She had a drink in her right hand and used the other to animate her words. Although the temperature outside was 75 degrees, if she fell in, the water was cold enough to shock her into a quick drowning, or within a few minutes, the same result by hypothermia. With the sails up and a 5-knot current, she might as well fall onto a sword. There would be little chance of getting her back on board alive.

"Hey, Abdel, could you please come here?"

"I can hear you, what's up?"

"I need you to get down from that rail."

"Don't worry, I'm a great swimmer."

Abdel was wearing a bathing suit. In an effort to feign falling in, she leaned backward far enough over the rail to win a Jamaican limbo contest. Instantly Brad was numb with fear. He had told all beforehand that there was a two-drink limit. As a responsible captain, he tried to monitor everyone's alcohol intake. Even if she wasn't drunk, she just might have been a free spirit who wanted to take a swim when she felt like one. He was afraid if he ordered Abdel sternly to come down, she might instinctively counteract his authority by trying to prove her swimming skills on that warm day. He had given a pre-sail speech, but the dangerous water temperature had not been part of it. He locked down the wheel and slowly moved toward her. It wasn't as if he could toss her a breathalyzer before deciding. He grabbed her leg with two hands as if both their lives depended on it.

"Please come down, the water is still freezing cold."

"OK, OK, but can you get your hands off my leg please."

"As soon as you're back on the deck."

With his hands still on her leg, she clumsily dropped back onto the deck surface a foot below with a thump, spilling her drink in the process. She was embarrassed and ticked off. He apologized profusely and did his best to explain the danger the water possessed. He prayed she understood, but it was clear that it did little to relieve the humiliation of that moment.

At the dock, everybody drank coffee. After a sail, Brad usually felt it necessary to be very an overly subservient host to his sailing novice guests. It was his way of compensating for the sometimes-necessary behavior of a captain underway. This was that to the extreme. Brad of course gave more attention to Abdel. He couldn't stop apologizing and trying to make light of the events. He kept at it, after he should have realized it was becoming patronizingly counterproductive. She said she understood, but it was easy to see that she didn't want to be near him. He made sure they had a designated driver for their trip home. After they left, Brad made a halfhearted attempt to rinse the salt off the teak; he dropped the hose on the deck.

He hurriedly went down below to pull himself together. Seated on his bunk after gathering his wits, he put himself on trial. He weighed all that had gone down. *Could I have kept my hands by her legs ready to grab, or sat up on the rail by her? . . . I could have missed a moving target, or with her momentum she might have slipped out of my grasp. If I sat by her, I could have gone in with her. Even if calling those viable options, my error was on the side of safety.*

Without rationalization, the verdict was in; he did what he had to do. He was mostly absolved. He just kicked himself for not precipitating the possibility of something like this happening and including it in his speech. He hoped Abdel would soon focus less on her ass bouncing off the deck in front of all and more on the rationale of his actions. Almost completely back to his pre-grabbing self, he drove the half mile to his house alone.

He was proud of his gentlemanly behavior with Melisa, yet regretful for passing up such an easy and lovely catch. A few moments later the doorbell rang. Say bye-bye to good intentions, and hello to Brad and Melisa.

Much of the sizing-up of his attraction to a mate would come in the seconds following the most physical part of the pairing. At that moment, his thoughts could range anywhere from *What the hell did I just do? How am I going to worm my way out of this one?* to *I hope I kept up my part of the bargain long enough.*

As the saying attributed to Woody Allen goes, "Sex is only dirty if done properly." Melisa was heavy on the proper, hold the prim. In short, she was a sweet country girl with a kinky streak. Aside from having the scholastic brains to graduate medical school, Melisa had a great read on almost everybody. The one foul and pugnacious exception was her best friend. Julie acted like her militant defender, and Melisa thought of her that way—in fact, bragged about her in that light. Julie once secretly offered Brad a massage date. Two hours after he politely declined her offer, she pointed out all his flaws to Melisa. He subtly hinted at this and other similar incidents to Melisa, who laughed them off as beyond reality. Julie stayed by a boyfriend whose hugs were often initiated for the purpose of throwing her to the ground and some of whose touches came in the form of slaps.

Melisa: "Brad called me last Friday forty-five minutes after he was supposed to."

Julie: "It's only going to get worse; you need to dump his sorry ass now."

When Brad and Melisa traveled, she was open to his flirting with other women. The only caveat was that they agree upon the woman beforehand. As I assume most were hoping, they had a common goal in this. Other than the triangular results of a few of these approaches, the most enjoyable parts for Brad were, one, continuing doing what he felt born to do with other women (the best moments in his life were watching new conquests' panties slide off their hips) and two, watching the reaction on the target's face and trying to translate her body language, as she began to understand the possible purpose of their attention. The cherry on top was that the woman knew what she was limited to getting and was owed no more than that—*My deepest apologies, for leaving it there; it wouldn't be part of the story.*

Brad had a habit of staring at attractive women. Despite her open orientation, Melisa was no fan of this.

"Oh, c'mon, Melisa. It's normal. All men do it."

"No, they don't."

"All the guys I know stare, at least every once in awhile."

"My father never did."

"Not even once?"

"Nope."

"Oh, please! In all the years, not even one time?"

"OK, but just once."

"Details please."

"My younger brother brought home this gorgeous seventeen-year-old girl; I mean drop-dead gorgeous. Everybody but my mother couldn't keep their eyes off of her. My mom got pretty upset and brought dad into the kitchen where I was, and then went off on him."

"What did he say?"

"Well, maw yah sure gotta admit, she's good looking."

Melisa regretted giving him the perfect get-out-of-jail-free card that, when called for, he recited, accent and all, over and over.

As per Melisa's hinting, he was considering marrying her, but hesitated because of a few red flags. Her friend Julie phoned the house six or seven times a day. Often, well before the time she had previously been told that Melisa was expected to return. As a result, he walked around his own home with a nervous stomach affecting his sleep. Melisa informed Brad that her mother didn't like him. That declaration would have seemed more plausible if her mother had already met him. She just went on the word of the yap-happy Julie. When he finally did meet her mom, she was rude to him. Time and his continued respect changed nothing. Brad was not all that bothered by it. *I'm not planning on marrying her mother, and there's 339 miles of DMZ between us.*

His own moral code wouldn't let him return fire or often even defend himself. Brad thought he loved Melisa. What concerned him was that Melisa made no attempt to rein in Julie or her mom. Being subjected to those outside agitators without her stepping between was Southern fried food for thought. And enough of it, to keep the engagement ring in a holding pattern.

The three times Brad and Melisa traveled to New York, they stayed with his stockbroker friend. Bill owned a regally decorated three-bedroom apartment off Central Park West. When he visited Charleston, he stayed with them. Through his guidance, Brad's savings had been growing at a better-than-market rate. At dinner with Brad and Melisa in New York, Bill spoke about a well-capitalized technology company with a tremendous upside. He and his new partner in a small brokerage house, Sam Ackerman, were personally invested in it. This was 1996, shortly after the birth of the first tech boom. Sam was also heavily involved on the promotional side of the tech company, in ways that Brad didn't bother to try to understand, and in ways Sam made sure nobody understood. Brad was doing well enough in all his other investments, so he didn't give any of the hype much consideration.

He paid more attention to his brisket sandwich until Melisa stated, "My dad just received a workman's comp settlement and his pension in one lump sum; we could use some advice."

Bill saw little risk with the company and began pointing more of his dialogue at her. Later that evening in bed, she asked Brad what his thoughts were on it.

"I've always known Bill to be honest, especially from a risk-assessment standpoint. We've been friends a long time; he's not going to hide anything. That being said, why would your dad, in his position, take any risk? I mean, if he were to buy in, he shouldn't invest any more than he could afford to lose, which doesn't sound like a lot. This is something different. I don't know who this new guy Ackerman is. I trust Bill's judgment in people, but still. Please don't do anything with them on the count of my friendship with him. Your mom and dad have to realize where they are financially and move real slowly with anything that is not FDIC insured."

Brad fell asleep early, while Melisa and Bill chatted in the kitchen for an hour. The next morning Melisa informed Brad that she was going to buy a few thousand dollars of the stock. She did and tripled her money within a month. Unbeknownst to Brad until after the fact, Melisa's dad, on seeing his daughter's windfall, jumped in. As Bill was on vacation, Ackerman handled the transaction. In the frenzy of the times, he encouraged him to put in what amounted to half of his savings. Brad called Bill trying to find out why his partner, who supposedly knew the connection, would let an unsophisticated investor go all in on one stock.

"I pulled the commission."

"OK, I appreciate that, but didn't Ackerman feel him out as to how much was safe for him to invest?"

"He did, but the guy wanted in bad. I wouldn't be that worried; our analysts are calling this one a winner. That's what they do all day. They're experts."

"What experts? Ackerman dropped this guy off in the Vegas without strippers. I'm picturing some nerd jerk-off flying around in a new helicopter, playing big shot with the money this guy literally broke his back for. Can you call him up and talk him into selling or at least diversifying?"

"Consider it done. Ackerman has his ear, so I'll tell him to call the guy first thing in the morning."

Bill did, and implored Ackerman to do as Brad had instructed.

Ackerman: "You know the guy is going to blame me for the rest of his life when this stock goes through the roof."

Bill: "Tell me what he'll think of you, me, and Brad if the bottom falls out? My buddy is ready to marry his daughter, for Christ's sake! Do you need me to explain to you the ramifications for Brad and me, if this thing tanks? This tech business is too new to us. These stocks are overvalued by any parameters we've spent our lives going by."

Ackerman: "We've been agreeing all along; this tech business is different, and we're gonna miss the boat if we're not jumping on it now."

Bill: "This is my best friend's future family; don't fuck around, don't fuck with me here. You spread that motherfucker out!"

Ackerman called Melisa's dad and made a quarter-hearted attempt, which had its intended non-effect. He told Bill,

"It's in the process, but the guy is fighting me hard."

Illicit self-interest is a bitch and just turned Brad's world into one. Unbeknownst to Brad, Melisa, her dad, and even Bill, Ackerman—via a side deal—was on the cusp of receiving an inordinately large kicker or bonus from the tech company. He just had to exceed a certain quarterly target. (That treachery wasn't exposed until seven years after the fact.) Brad, through Melisa and Bill, followed up a few times to see if he had lessened his position. He received little in the way of an answer and finally butted out. He was left to wishing that her dad hadn't chosen to take his pension in a lump sum.

Melisa's family stayed in Brad's house after Melisa's dad—on Brad's dime—was medevacked out of his upstate hospital and into a better-equipped Charleston cardiac unit. He'd had a massive heart attack. Seated in the waiting area of the intensive care unit three days after surgery, Brad, Melisa, her mom, her sister, and Julie saw a priest walking down the hallway. With rubber legs, zombie like, they all followed him. He stopped to read the name on the chart attached to the door of Melisa's father's room. As soon as he did, the hand not wrapped in his cross's chain carefully pushed it open. Through that space, they no longer heard the intermittent beeps that had steadied them the last few days. Now they listened to the translation of God's pronouncement via the steady shrill of a flat line.

Melisa's mom looked at Brad and barely squeaked out, "How could you have let this happen?"

As if she had used her last drop of air to say it, she collapsed. Nurses gently pulled Melisa away as they began to treat her mom for shock. Melisa and her nineteen-year-old sister embraced and sobbed. More nurses stood by them prepared to give support if needed. Julie stuck both her middle fingers in Brad's face. He only blamed himself. His character would not let him instantly pardon his responsibility with facts. His self-worth had never been lower, yet it still towered above the worth of the tech stock. That paper was now worth about the price of the dinners Brad had paid for over the last three days. The stock never rebounded. After a heart stoppage of almost a minute, followed by a week on life support, Melisa's father did.

Bill and Brad's friendship, while strained during the ordeal, stayed intact. Brad knew full well his friend's heart was in the right place. Melisa's parents counted on her to help them with business decisions. They were ready to sue. Brad had spoken with two lawyer friends. Given the known facts, they both said it was not a great case to take on. Her parents would have a hard time finding someone to do so, solely on a percentage basis. Brad could not fathom encouraging a lawsuit against his buddy who went in with only good intentions. Melisa asked Brad for his thoughts.

Rather than stay completely neutral, he said, "Listen, Ackerman is fully deserving of somebody making him dead. He's a heartless and greedy prick. The thing is, you would have to sue them both. Bill removed the commission once he learned who the sale was to, and he ordered Ackerman to convince you're dad to diversify his investment. Bill bought into Ackerman's pleas of innocence that weren't. I'm convinced he was blind to whatever Ackerman was pulling. On the other hand, clearly they're going to need money, so this is a decision they have to make."

Eight years after the fact, the New York papers wrote an expose on Ackerman and his numerous scams. The Securities and Exchange Commission barred him for life. Melisa could never bring herself to be in the company of Bill again. Her mom and Julie's venom aimed at Brad increased to intolerable levels. Melisa justly held him mostly blameless on what happened to her father. The lack of his complete neutrality concerning the lawsuit stuck with her, and even more so with him. Brad never forgave Julie for being Julie. He understood her mother's words in the hospital were spoken in the depths of an intense pain. Yet now he couldn't fathom a future with her mother and Julie even near it. That, combined with Melisa pushing for a marriage, overstressed a guy who had never entertained the idea before her. Melisa and Brad held on for another six months, until Brad called the deal off. By all accounts, they weren't enjoying each other's company. He couldn't understand why she cried so hard.

Julie was not aware the day they broke up and called the house.

"She's not here, buh-bye!" Click!

A book could be written on just that—*The Joy of Hanging Up*. With the phone comatose on its charging stand, he lay on his bed the following days in such a peaceful state; it was as if he was levitating.

Safe Harbor

Brad had been living in Charleston for seven years. He was

now thirty-eight and had lost interest in dating women under twenty-eight or twenty-nine. He made friends with some younger but limited it to only that. He thought he could serve them better by being a mentor. Passing along a free meal and insights into the mind-sets of the guys who were the cause of most of their issues was often rewarding. Never mind that he was short on good company. Relegating them to the no-go zone was also frustrating, as he felt a few might have been a good match with the addition of five or so years. After establishing these friendships, he didn't want to risk a transition into something that would put wear and tear on them. The do-gooder method of mingling with the opposite sex did little to relieve his loneliness and fear for his future.

Finding a more seasoned mate who hadn't or wouldn't soon get wind of his various titles (womanizer, serial dater, noncommittal) had become near impossible. The enveloping gossip had reduced him to what was paramount to house arrest. He played table hockey with buddies and walked his dogs until they begged out. Dry spells beget longer dry spells. His attitude toward life was the least positive it had ever been. To break the monotony of his evenings, he began going to yoga classes given at a karate dojo not far from his house. Brad was too respectful of women's privacy to approach them at the beach or the gym, let alone at a predominantly female yoga class. He was careful to always place his mat in the front, to avoid even the suspicion of staring. He even limited the use of the mirrors for that purpose. The teacher was a finely crafted specimen of all that he lusted for in a woman. She was thirty-three years old, a solid 5'10" with the toned physique that goes along with job. She was polite, kind, and kept a professional distance from all. The latter made her all the more attractive to Brad. She gave him a little more personal attention than the others. Although self-conscious about it, he was flattered when she would help bend him to get into a pose. He was never sure if there was an attraction on her part or if it was simply because he needed the extra help. Either way, he held a healthy respect for her. He said and did nothing that could be construed as even a veiled come-on.

Although most of the students were close to his age, he saw himself as different from most. Many were vegetarians, some studied eastern philosophies and all that goes with that. To his way of thinking, even if they talked about it more, they had no better idea about how the world should be than anybody else. Nevertheless, as most of the students chatted after class, he slowly became friendly with some of the practitioners. There was a couple that seemed to enjoy talking with him. He came to know a few married women who came to the class mostly alone. As Brad was the newest regular, one guy went out of his way to be welcoming. Slowly it dawned on him that this group passed little in the way of gossip. It became his sanctuary; hidden from the Charleston he was all too familiar with. He increasingly came to value his time there and the people he met.

After eight months, he thought to invite his yoga class friends—including the husbands—to his house for a dinner party. He tried to be discreet so that others wouldn't overhear. As he was mentioning this to the couple, he realized the teacher was directly behind him. Although not on his list, he now felt obligated to invite her also. He did so as casually as possible; she accepted. No one there knew much about him. He had sold the Vette and was now driving an SUV. As he was no longer living on the boat, it was easier not to mention it to anyone in class. He wanted to appear down-to-earth and blend in. Eastern religions aside, his ego was toning down. Except for the teacher's, he didn't find the dinner conversation exhilarating. Still, he was glad to show his appreciation for their acceptance of him.

Even more so than sanding and varnishing the teak, the hardest part of his owning the boat was playing social director. Sharing the experience of sailing in a confined space for an afternoon often leads to friendships. If you bring a person one day and the whole crew got tight, people will sometimes wonder why they weren't included in the next outing. Never mind the acquaintances that never got invited. The boat became a social burden. He never once mentioned it to anyone in the school.

Through the mirrors, he spotted a tall, highly attractive redhead of thirty-one who came to only one other class months earlier. As he was leaving, he noticed her walking fifteen feet behind him. He took baby steps in the hopes of her catching up. They were parked alongside each other. Even if their meeting didn't, conversation began naturally. Rhonda mentioned she was partners in a tiny, rustic Cajun restaurant on the outskirts of town. Less for the gumbo, he went for lunch a day later. She sat down at his table. Her long hair, though clean, was neglected. She wore a potato sack–shaped sundress that at least had the decency of being short enough to see her stunning long legs. Those alone were enough to believe that all points north were their equal. They got on well in a reserved way. He admired her for coming off so calmly during their conversations, while still having an eye out to make sure all was in order. Over the next few months, he downed half a dozen shrimp creoles and jambalayas.

Slowly, he was getting Rhonda's story. She had a boyfriend, "sort of." She grew up middle class in San Diego, with one sister. At the age of fifteen, her father divorced her mom. He had hired a lawyer better than someone in his position typically would. Her mom settled for numbers even less than commensurate with his furniture-salesman income. He neglected to tell her during the negotiation that he had an uncle in Seattle who was dying of cancer. That might not seem pertinent, if not for another omitted detail: the childless widower was planning to leave him a successful beer distributorship. Soon thereafter cancer won, and her dad, now single, moved north as a rich man. After he paid off the agreed-upon two installments, which he laughed off as chump change, he sent no more money for the girls. Within a year, he remarried, and within two more, he had a baby daughter and son. Whether or not he had good reasons to leave his first wife, only he knows. As to why he completely abandoned his thirteen- and fifteen-year-old daughters . . . well, that fact alone should make you not want to get close enough to ask. Brad, after hearing this, empathized with Rhonda—and shortly thereafter slept with her.

Their pre-, during-, and post-coital chatter was nothing out of the ordinary; perverse as should be. For instance, they had asked each other to rate, in order, the top three people at yoga class they would like to do. Brad went first, and put the teacher at number one. Rhonda had her at number two. That proclivity was news to him. He kind of suspected she had that attribute but wasn't all that keyed up about pursuing it. He was open to the idea, but having just been there, it was mostly out of his system. He was now less about playing and more about finding a life partner. He never hinted about being included, nor did she. *Those deals normally work better, if the guy plays the opposite of salesman anyways.* Brad wasn't an exhibitionist, yet he was glad that a buddy of his who was between apartments was occupying the room directly across the hall. If her head wasn't bouncing off the headboard, she made sure his was. Her sex was a scratching, slapping, biting, and screaming affair; scary by the sound of it. He continued partly because she was completely different outside of the bedroom. The fact that someone else was witnessing her coming back for more of the same was insurance enough to continue on this ride. Her style of lovemaking, entertaining in its energetic way, was off-putting in another sense. He wasn't sure he wanted to spend much more time looking and feeling like he had replaced his yoga mat with a section of barbed wire fence.

She began to come to class a little more frequently. He was up to eating at her restaurant twice a week. He tried to only be served by a certain twenty-three-year-old waitress. You have reason to, but don't jump to conclusions: she was plain in appearance and personality. Even if not entangled with her boss, he would have had no sexual interest in her. They made little conversation. Still, he was drawn to her in the way one would be to a helpless puppy. He enjoyed overtipping her for that reason. He came to feel they had a mutual admiration society. They unabashedly tossed uplifting vibes each other's way. He took so many people from yoga there, it soon became a hangout for many from his class.

He once invited a fifty-year-old pulmonary doctor confidant there. Malcolm and Brad had met at the marina and regularly sailed on each other's boats. He admired the doctor and wanted him to meet Rhonda. Malcolm dug the hippie-like atmosphere of the place. He had served as a medic in Vietnam and, although having an offbeat motorcycle-riding lifestyle, was highly thought of in Charleston for his charity work. At one lunch, there was a hair in Malcolm's soup. Overly respectful of Brad's connection to the place, he wasn't going to send it back, nor was he planning on eating it. Seeing that, Brad took it on himself to point it out to his waitress friend. She replaced the soup.

Another day Brad came in for lunch; he spotted Rhonda standing with a guy. When Brad walked over, "Oh hey, Brad, I'd like you to meet my boyfriend, Austin."

"Hey, Austin, nice to meet you."

"Nice to meet you too, Brad."

Austin's round cheeks glowed in the company of Rhonda. He was about her height, on the chubby side, wearing khakis, a dress shirt, and deck shoes, by threads, a typical Charlestonian. At least looks-wise, he was clearly overachieving by snagging Rhonda. Animated and jovial without pushing his personality too hard, he was immediately likeable. Brad felt he was being given extra respect, if not bowed to, because he was a friend of hers. *Eeesssh-ouch!* He didn't appear to be the type to play battlefield-bed, as she required of Brad. Maybe she needed different lovers for different functions. Then again . . . insert book-cover cliché here. Although Rhonda had mentioned she had a "sort of" boyfriend that one time, it didn't help much to lessen the weirdness of the moment. Playing the friend role in their company was aided by the way Austin came off: a decent and genuine guy. If he really wasn't, knew the score and was just a sly competitor. It still appeared like he loved her; Brad was sure he didn't. Thus, he knew the last time he had slept with Rhonda would be exactly that, the last time. After being told in so many words that he rated no higher than second fiddle, he drove away feeling smaller. Three stoplights later, all he felt was grateful for the escape clause. He didn't call her, and she never contacted him.

The next few weeks, his fantasies refocused on the yoga teacher. The only reason they had strayed was he thought her to be unattainable. I doubt I'm breaking new ground for anybody with the following. A guy can run up numbers with women for various reasons. It's not always a sign of confidence; often enough it signals the opposite. Although not conscious of it, Rhonda was a cop-out, a distraction for him to hide from his feelings for the teacher. He would be defenseless with her if they hooked up. There was no game to her. She looked, moved, and behaved exactly as he dreamed a woman should. He was awed. For that reason, he feared her. He had been going to her class for over a year. Her conversation at the one dinner at his house was straightforward and insightful. Unlike him, she mostly asked questions of others and only spoke about herself when asked to. Without knowing her intimately, if she would have walked up to him and said you are going to spend the rest of your life with me, he would have fallen to his knees and kissed her feet. She was, in every sense of how he defined the word, a goddess.

Brad believed his and Rhonda's relationship was never known in class. At her restaurant, they were careful not to tip their shared hat. Brad hadn't mentioned it to anyone in class, and the fact that he didn't even rate a "sort of" boyfriend led him to believe she would have kept their fling to herself. He hadn't seen Rhonda in class since meeting Mr. "Sort of." He assumed she was embarrassed about what had happened with Austin. Regardless of that, as she was so nice, he had the urge to call and tell her why he couldn't go on. *Hey, Rhonda, after meeting Austin, and him being such a cool guy and so nice to me, I would feel like an even bigger heel than I did then, if we continued.*

Pride took over, and his thoughts moved to, *why do I owe that bitch a call? If she asked me to play eunuch in front of tubby Señor "Sort of boyfriend," I'm not anything to her. Fuck her; she's the one who owes me a call.*

As if he were talking to a mirror, *What the fuck is wrong with you, feeling all guilty when you have nothing to feel guilty about? . . . Well, not with her anyhow.*

In class, Brad chatted with the regulars; all was the same. When the teacher touched him to manipulate his position, the thrill was not of a base sexuality. He felt as his loving mongrel did when Brad returned home from a trip. It was a pure happiness from the inside out. The joy of being handled by her in such a caring way spoke to his soul better than any cheap thrill ever did. Well, maybe that's pushing it a little. He wanted to become friends, yet words were hard to come by. If he ever could get a friendship going, and she wanted more, she would have to take it there. He couldn't risk hurting the person who, without her knowing it, brought him more pleasure than anything else in his life. He thought it best to wait to be sure the coast was all clear from the Rhonda affair before an attempt. As months went by, before trying to enunciate them, his many scripts would stutter away into oblivion. In an almost imperceptible way, he somewhere between hoped and sensed that she understood he was fighting to break through. There was no doubt this would be one pose he would have to bend to move into on his own. She was flawless; he felt too far from that to pass through her aura of goodness.

A Yoga Stretch for Brad's Sanity

Before class one evening, Brad had taken only a few steps from his car when he was approached by the owner of the karate studio and the yoga teacher. They circled him with their fists balled, their heart rates elevated. The owner looked at him as if ready to strike. Totally caught off guard and confused, Brad turned to the yoga teacher, and she looked just as ready to do the same. He looked back at the owner, who said, "You can't come in here anymore."

"Why not?"

"We have five women that will come forward to say you either raped them or abused them."

"Whaaat? . . . This is a mistake. You have me confused with someone else. This makes no sense."

Brad looked away and noticed that all of the roughly twenty people in the class were standing by the floor-to-ceiling windows, watching. All those he noticed had either an angry or an admonishing look. He could think of nothing more to say. He got back in his car and drove home. His sanctuary was instantly transformed into a wrung of hell he wasn't familiar with. On the drive, he felt sick to his stomach. That feeling gave way when his mind separated from the body in the driver's seat. He couldn't organize his thoughts. He was as shattered as he had ever been. In shock, it was a miracle that he made it home without tasting his steering wheel. After an hour of fighting to regain his wits, he tried to think who these accusers could be. The only one he could think of was the wack job Rochelle. *That was close to two years ago, why would she do something so evil and dangerous? I did nothing to her . . . Or was that was the problem? Four other people, this is nuts. If I look in the mirror tomorrow morning and all I see is Kafka's cockroach, it might come as a relief.*

He called a lawyer buddy of his from Houston, who got angry on his behalf, "Tell them to call the police then!"

That was the most satisfying answer he received from the guy friends he called. The others appeared to be wondering what he really did. Some insinuated and others outright said he must have treated them roughly for them to level such serious accusations. No better time than in a crisis to learn who your friends are. That following day he called the school and spoke with the owner.

"Roger, I think we need to talk."

"So talk."

"I'd like a chance to defend myself. If you tell me who they are, I can tell you my side of the story."

"I'm not going to give you their names so you can intimidate and harass them."

"I'm not going to harass anyone, or even speak with anyone. I assure you, I'm more afraid of them than they are of me . . . OK then, just tell me what these people said I did, and at least let me give you my side. I never abused or raped anybody. Do you think it's fair to deny me the right to give my side of the story? By doing so, you're helping to spread the word all over town that I'm a rapist. I am the furthest thing from that! If you're not going to do anything to help me clear this up, then encourage them to go to the police. I don't want these lies hanging over my head. I hope you understand they are destroying my life. I'm guilty of being naïve and probably insensitive, but nothing more."

"Let me think about it."

Brad's next course of action was to ask previous girlfriends to call or go to the karate school and speak with the owner on his behalf. This absurdity had to be corrected as soon as possible. Although not a girlfriend but rather a hangout buddy, he called Betty who had introduced him to Rochelle. He told her what happened, certain her friend Rochelle was one of the five. He saw no point in wondering how she could have passed this on to his yoga crowd. Six degrees of separation would be an overstatement by four degrees. Everybody knows everybody in the downtown area. If Charleston ever grew to surpass Mexico City in population, its citizens' perpetually moving mouths would keep it a small town. The only thing they'd need to learn to do is talk faster.

"Betty, you told me her sister said she likes to fight. Do you know anything more that could help me?"

"No."

"There must be more you could learn from her or her sister to help me. I wouldn't ask you to do that if this wasn't such a serious situation."

"I'm more friends with her sister than Rochelle; I can't be a spy for you. You don't even know for sure she was one of them."

"If I find out that she was, can you try to help me?"

"Let me think about it."

She told the truth. She did think about it, nothing more.

Melisa and Brad chatted every few weeks. He was still concerned for her and her family, especially her dad. He called and asked what was happening in her life. This time he was too busy organizing all that he was ready to blurt out, to pay much attention to her. He hoped to get her small talk out of the way as quickly as manners would permit. In spite of his concentration being on himself, he thought he picked up on something within her that was off, distant. He knew her well.

Did she find somebody new and, as a result, want to push me out of the picture altogether? Did she meet her quota of being nice to the ex and want not to be reminded of me?

He began to worry that she was hiding news about her dad, or anything that could have brought more sadness into her life. After she calmed his fears, he then unloaded his news. She had little to say in response. He appreciated her sympathy; the story shocked her into a stunned silence.

He asked her if she could speak with the owner. Her hesitancy surprised him. She wouldn't commit. He had dropped all else in his life for a month during and after her dad's surgery. He also expended a good bit of money on her family in their time of crisis. He was fast learning that people don't jump into sticky situations quickly.

Maybe I pitched her too hard. I didn't marry her; I disappointed her, and then dumped her.

A few days later, Melisa called the owner and spoke with him. She then called Brad and told him that she had done so. Finally, he was starting to right this wrong!

Right after speaking with Melisa the first time, he thought the person even better to speak up for him was Rhonda. Plenty from his school ate and hung out at her restaurant. They all either knew her, or of her. Obviously, she must have had heard about this. They hadn't been in contact, and he was worried she might harbor a grudge. When he phoned and told her what happened, she was also sympathetic and appeared nervous for him. She had little to say but was a good listener.

"I understand you have a boyfriend and might not want to divulge too much about us, but could you say something to the effect, that we have been good buddies for awhile. And if you believe me when I tell you this is all a bunch of bull, please tell them I'm nothing like that, and incapable of doing something like that. Don't let me put words in your mouth, but if you could help in any way I'd really appreciate it . . . I know this might sound and be self-serving at this point, but I was sorry I didn't explain why I stopped calling. After meeting Austin, and seeing how happy he acted around you, I didn't want to be the one to mess that up. Even if I had been with you first, I would have had to weigh my feelings for you pretty seriously after watching him around you."

"I'll try."

Brad had recently become acquainted with a small theater owner with whom he had been discussing going in as his partner on another one. Brad knew crying about his situation to everybody would only make it worse. He had to choose his ears carefully. This guy had struck him as intelligent and worldly. Blabbing here might screw up the deal they were discussing. As they were in the midst of business talks, in which he had no plans to drop his story; it streamed out of him as if he were talking to a shrink.

His new friend's assessment: "The new rooster in the henhouse."

Those six words said so much. His new friend instantly believed him and at the same time gave the discombobulated Brad a good reason as to how and why this happened.

He decided to go on the offensive and received a recommendation for a lawyer. He told her about his case without interruption for five minutes.

"Why not just suck it up."

"Excuse me?"

"I've driven by that place; who are we going to sue, and for what damages? A guy with garish hand-painted murals on the outside of his rented dump, a yoga teacher, and five people that might cost you money to learn who they are? That would be a waste of my time and your money."

Roger wasn't savvy enough to fear the legal ramifications of his actions. He had discussed the situation with his wife, and she had told him the right thing to do was to hear Brad's side. Brad felt degraded but saw no other way out other than to defend himself to this duped and hostile person. He tried to understand that Roger's motivation was about protecting the women. He saw no other viable choice. His school had become a major conduit in spreading these lies. The most painful insult was not that all these Lilliputians could judge him this way, but to his deceased parents. In essence, they were being accused of raising a person capable of this.

"Hey, Brad, I'm calling you to hear your side of the

story. Not sure what you could possibly tell me to change things. So many people have come forward that everybody believes this is true."

"Roger, I appreciate the call and you having the courage to step into the middle of this mess. Let me respond first to what 'everybody believes' this way. There are certain parts of our state where everybody seems to think Jim and Tammy Faye Baker are the prophets of God; does that make it true?"

"OK."

"You don't even have to let me know if I have the right person. I'm going to say her name and tell you exactly what happened. If I'm guessing who this person is correctly, and you have any belief in what I say, probably best to have a woman friend question her about it. Or the person she told it to. Then ask around about her. I don't believe I'm the first guy she had problems of this nature with. I met Rochelle through a mutual friend . . ."

Brad spared no detail when he recited verbatim what had happened. He spoke as if it occurred yesterday. Every word he enunciated traveled directly from his heart to the phone pressed against Roger's ear. Roger was in his late thirties; he'd had his own experiences with some crazies. This recounting opened his mind, but he still had serious doubts, as there had been all the others with their own claims.

"Did my ex-girlfriend Melisa speak with you on my behalf?"

"I spoke with her, and she said you never physically hurt her, but you were emotionally abusive."

The 210-pound karate instructor had nothing more lethal in his arsenal than the gut punch just landed on Brad. After quickly gathering his wits, Brad's tone changed, his words came out slowly, and from a softer region of the heart. He once loved her and still did in many ways.

"Look, Roger, I don't know how much right I have to speak to you about our year and a half relationship, but I can tell you this: I never once yelled at her. I never demeaned her in any way that I can think of. Maybe I kidded her on something she took the wrong way, I don't know. If she did take something I did or said that badly to call it abuse, I can tell you honestly, I would feel terrible. In fact, I do now on hearing this. Many times, in the relationship, I felt it was the other way around. I was the one taking the pounding. She would make fun of different things about me looks-wise. Maybe I didn't compliment her enough. We went through a very serious personal situation together that I can't speak about. I feel I could have handled it better, but I don't see how it could in any way be construed as emotional abuse. I'm not on the phone to defend how good a boyfriend I was or wasn't, but if by her accusation she means that I intentionally meant to hurt her, it's not true. The breakup was hard on both of us; I'm guessing more so for her. Maybe I could have handled that better also. If she feels so harmed as to say that I was emotionally abusive, it's likely I was insensitive in various ways I didn't realize. Would not be the first time I've heard that."

The last sentence rang true for Roger also, and good luck in finding a guy who hasn't heard that. Roger was just beginning to feel that maybe he had been misled. His guard came down a little more and he continued, "A waitress in a student's restaurant said you told her there was a pubic hair in your soup."

Another shot landed that had Brad wincing. The sting was in the betrayal from his little pretend friend. This one was more easily countered. His voice returned to the offensive.

"Absolutely not true, let me tell you exactly what did happen. Thank God I have a witness to prove this one away. I went to lunch with my friend Dr. Malcolm Walsh. He's a fifty-year-old Vietnam vet. Half the work he does is for charity. Go try and find a better-respected and well-liked guy in Charleston. He knew I went to the place a lot, so he was hesitant to tell her there was a hair in his soup. I was friends with the waitress. At least I thought I was. I held the bowl up to show her and spoke for Malcolm. 'There's a hair in this soup.' A hair, just a hair, nothing more. Do you want his phone number. Do you want me to ask him to see you tomorrow? Let me tell you, I'm happy I can wipe that lie away easy, but this hurts bad. I was nothing but nice to that girl. Never once bitched about anything to her. I can be impatient, but I never was with her. I liked her, and I thought she liked me. I had no designs on her; I just dug the positive vibes we passed each other. Total and complete bullshit!"

Roger was now beginning to realize he had been duped by a gaggle of women with axes to grind. They took a break from the phone trial and spoke on unrelated subjects. As Roger worked with the yoga teacher and was friends with her, he felt it necessary to clear the air on one more accusation. It was as hard for him to ask the next question as it was for Brad to hear and answer it.

"Did you tell anyone that you wanted fuck Susan, the yoga teacher?"

Brad continued quietly with difficulty; his voice perceptibly pained.

"Yes, I did . . . and I now regret saying it more than you might think. I hope you will give me a chance to explain a little more. If you heard this, I don't feel a need to protect Rhonda's privacy, because obviously it came from her. Rhonda and I had a thing for a few weeks. I had a friend staying at my house that can back that up. I broke it off for what I thought was a valid reason. I said it during a bedtime game we played. We would ask each other who we'd like to do from class. It was in-bed sex talk. Sometimes we'd be doing it when we named these people. We played it a few times. I believe I used the words 'to do,' not fuck. I will apologize to her if you think she would be OK with it."

Roger's words blurted out as if he had no control over them. "All rules are off in bed."

He was furious that she would take Brad's words so far out of context. He was equally angry for Rhonda not disclosing their relationship, as the stew pot of vindictiveness was stirred to a boil in her restaurant. He became even more livid realizing he was complicit in this witch-hunt, fueled by a pack of lies.

"Obviously, she didn't talk about us in bed to you, but if for any reason she attacks me again, trust this, we did it how she wanted it, not me, all that much anyways."

"If what you say is true, she is one seriously mean-spirited woman."

Brad interrupted him, "Listen Roger, I'm not really in the mood to defend her, but let me say this anyways. She was a very nice person in the time I spent with her. I'm only telling you this to cool both our jets. I don't want to see her business damaged. I don't want to be the cause of any more acrimony. I hope you will keep this private, as it might be personal to her—I'm not sure if it is, but just the same I think I have a moral reason to tell it to you: When she was fifteen, her father took off and made a new family a few years later. He never called her again. In desperation, she did something she had never done. She rifled through her mother's belongings to help locate him. She finally got him on the phone and cried about why he never called, and her dad answered, 'Ask your cunt mother why!' And then he slammed the phone down. That was her last conversation with him. He died in a car wreck three years later. I never thought of this until hearing you being upset with her, which in whatever way is because of me. She likely has some serious abandonment issues. I might have saved everybody a lot of grief if I had picked up on that earlier and not left her cold, regardless of my reasons."

"Let me speak to the people involved and get back with you."

"Thanks."

Taking the Wind Out of the Sails

As Rochelle's was the most serious charge, and only her word against his, Roger's first call was to the couple who Brad was friendly with in the class. They relayed to him that Janice, the woman of the couple, worked with Rochelle at a dentist's office. Two years earlier, Janice brought up his name to Rochelle in conversation about single and available guys she knew. Rochelle had routinely pushed to be fixed up. The second Janice spoke Brad's name, in all her victimized glory, Rochelle launched into a ten-minute, detailed and convoluted recounting.

A short summary: "He was so sweet at first. He invited me for one drink on his yacht, promising to take me home right after. When we passed the marina, where it was supposed to be, he said that he forgot he had lent it to a friend and said, 'Let's just go to my house; it's close.' When we got there, he offered me a tour of his place. Once in his bedroom, he pushed me on the bed and forced himself on me. I screamed for him to stop countless times."

Janice replied, "Why didn't you go to the police?"

"I was so messed up after I got out of his car, I just

wanted to take a shower. After I did, I was afraid after washing away the evidence; it would be just my word against his. I didn't want to be part of a scandal."

The story was at first shocking but soon sounded peculiar and far-fetched to Janice, especially as Brad was always so lighthearted and friendly. Janice had long since sized up Rochelle as an oddball. Janice only mentioned it, without going into its details, because she was sitting at a table with Rhonda and Melisa. Rhonda was talking about some crude thing he had said to one of her waitresses, and Melisa was railing about him being a bad guy. I found it all hard to believe."

Roger asked Janice if she could question Rochelle about what she told her, now two years later. Harm had come to Brad, and if this story wasn't true they, were part of the unjust cause. At lunch out of the office, she brought it up. Rochelle became defensive and wasn't her glib self; she knew it had landed center stage. After some prodding, Rochelle went into it again. Janice thought herself a brilliant detective, as the two stories had little in common—other than they were both lies. Janice called Roger and told him this. Susan went out to Rhonda's restaurant and confronted her. Fortunately, Brad had called Rhonda right after the storm began and explained why he stopped calling. Thereafter she lost all her motivation to demonize him. She quickly backpedaled off the nonsense she had promoted. Roger in turn had a talk with everybody in class. He called Brad and told him that his story checked out and it would be OK for him to come back to class.

"I don't think I would be comfortable there anymore, thanks just the same."

The original accusers had been questioned by a few of those who'd been misled and duped. Not one of them or the second generation of accusers they spawned had apologized to Brad.

Oh, and the part about Melisa sitting with Rhonda . . . no degrees of separation left there. And right as Brad's problem was beginning!

The Day-Care Center Pedophiles Epilogue

Why Brad owned a gun for a short time in Houston: A tile factory had given the twenty-two-year-old Brad a job to run their outdoor yard where they sold overruns and seconds. He put up a thirty-foot sign along the fence: TILE ONE ON YOURSELF. Sales boomed in the mostly cash business. Although it was in what was a bad neighborhood, it seemed like a tree-lined paradise to Brad. He had recently left the New York City of the late-1970s. On a busy day, while Brad was writing out a receipt, a cop in his fifties walked into his poorly lit trailer office.

With no other words spoken beforehand, he asked, "Do you have a gun?"

Brad slowly raised his open hands to ear level, not exactly sure why the officer was asking.

"No sir, no sir, I don't."

"Then, son, yah ought go git one."

In New York City, excluding law enforcement, owning a gun was a foreign concept to the vast majority of non-criminals. Even if you wanted one, you'd have to prove a good reason and jump through bureaucratic hoops to obtain a license for it. The idea struck him as *Dirty Harry* cool, so he went out and bought one with his driver's license. Soon it scared him to have it in the house. He never brought it to work and only used it a few times at a target range before selling it.

The why and how of him attempting to kill someone

goes like this: He was visiting his grandmother in Miami. She wanted to go out to dinner at a certain seafood joint. To get there, they had to pass through a few neighborhoods. One was in a quiet at this hour, industrial zone. Brad had a white rental car. In those days, the rental companies via the state government had not yet removed the Z from the license plates. To law enforcement, the Z signified it was a rental car. To criminals, that letter on the tag advertised a free lunch, carte blanche! They would stick up these cars with impunity. The rate and ferocity at which this was happening would make a stagecoach going through the worst outlaw territory in the Wild West appear safer than a children's ride at Disneyland. Back then, many of Miami's tourists were from Germany; others were from the northeastern United States and Canada. The percentage of these visitors who would fly back for a trial was minuscule. Why bother wasting time and money? They knew many of the offenders were juveniles and almost nothing would happen to them. At best they would be sent to a youth detention center, a quasi-training school with a clear career path: to become better and more well-rounded criminals. If they were already adults, the tourists' efforts would do little more than add another line on a typically long rap sheet.

Brad and his grandmother stopped at a red light. The pavement was wet from a quick shower two hours before. The road was undergoing construction; a little more than a yard to his left was a drop-off of at least a foot. A tall, skinny kid of about sixteen was crossing the street; when he reached a point midway between the headlights, he stopped and began waving a car antenna to appear like a crazy person, a distraction. The light turned green, the kid didn't move, he was staring off into space. Although Brad was highly suspicious of the kid, the ruse worked; he held

Brad's attention. Within a second, his grandmother's door was being opened by one of a team. Brad turned and saw him and another guy standing to his right holding a crowbar cocked and ready for action. If the door had been locked as it should have been, he would have swung the ten-pound bar to smash the window and likely his grandmother's face. Wherever the tool came to rest wouldn't have mattered to the criminal, if the window was gone. His concern was in popping the lock to gain entry and ease his job of grabbing her handbag. Thankfully the door was opened without that course of action. What came next wasn't instinctual. Brad made a conscious decision to run over the person in front of the car. He forced time enough to reason: it was his grandmother's life or the punk's. He slammed on the accelerator too hard. Other than the rear wheels, the car remained motionless for a second and a half. Then the back of the car skidded sideways to within a foot of the embankment before moving forward. Brad's heavy foot coupled with the slick pavement were likely the only two things that gave the kid time to jump away, to rob another day. As they drove off, they smiled at each other, passing each other telepathic high-fives. It wasn't until they were seated at their dinner table that their hearts began to pound and contemplate the other possible outcomes. He was eternally grateful for the rain that likely saved the kid's life.

Brad was sitting in front of his television in the wake of the rape firestorm that had been extinguished two days before. Trying to breathe through the smoke from it that he prayed would eventually blow away. Hoping to wash off the stains on his psyche, knowing he never completely could. He turned on the television and saw two long and weathered faces being interviewed. It was the Indian couple who had owned the day-care center. They had been incarcerated almost the entire time since he had watched the newscast about them eleven years earlier. They had been exonerated and recently released from jail. They were free, but with little hope of a worthwhile future. They knew the suspicions and stigma would never leave. They described their lives in prison, cast to the lower rungs of hell inside of it.

It went down like this: Two of the fathers, both psychologists brainwashed their kids to describe various perverse things that the couple did to them. By the time two fathers had done their work, their children could not have believed it more than if it really did happen. The government's expert interviewers had no doubt their stories were true. Then the other children were questioned. In those days, the interviewing methods were highly suspect, filled with leading questions that led to the children trying to please the adults and agree. They all did. With the reports in and the public opinion weighing so heavily against them, it's a miracle the vilified pair weren't buried alive before the trial. The reason the two California psychologists bent their kids' minds. The age-old story: it was about money. The school's insurance to be specific.

The television interviewer, after hearing the hell they went through in prison, the abandonment of friends and family, the lost years, asked, "Of all that you had to go through, what was the worst part of it?"

His wife nodded in agreement, as the husband stated, "Not one of the forty-five parents ever apologized."

Brad also nodded in agreement. Not one person from the yoga school or any of the piling-on conspirators had apologized to him.

Brad surmised out loud, "Of course they didn't; an apology proves you're admitting to and taking responsibility for a mistake or wrongdoing. It's safer for them to let things lie and leave an air of doubt as their moral out. On the other hand, if it would serve their own interests to offer them up, I might drown in them."

The best from Roger was, "You can come back to class."

As he was picking up the mail at his front door, he made eye contact with Janice and her husband. He walked back inside before an acknowledgment. Maybe they were afraid to, but they never rang the bell. Melisa remained in contact. He held no grudge; he felt he was owed it. When he ran into Rhonda a few months later, they chatted as if nothing had happened.

A week later, he walked into one of his regular haunts, a casual healthy downtown restaurant. He went to the counter to order food from the hip couple that owned the place. They had heard the story. They knew him and how polite he had always been with the staff, and the women he brought in. A year earlier he'd made conversation with the lady owner, as if she did not have a large cold sore on her mouth. Normally he never said much more than hello to her. From that day, they had even a higher degree of respect for him. He spotted a buddy of his. Willy was a chef who had come along on various offshore voyages as the cook. The actress his orthopedist friend had fixed him up with was the other person at his table. Willy asked him to join them. Brad reasoned, if he found his own table in the small place, Mandy might take it as an insult, so he sat down. Willy then went to the counter to refill his iced tea. The ex-actress, who of course had gotten wind of the story, entered stage left with, "You were so rough with me."

It wasn't because he was afraid to steal her scene; rather, he instantly realized his rejection many years back stung her anew with his presence. Hence, he vied for the table's Best Actor award.

"I'm very sorry you feel that way, Mandy. I never meant to be. I've always thought of you as a lovely person. If I wasn't myself, it was because I didn't feel good enough for you. The working L.A. actress thing intimidated me."

The curtain came down. Three months later, Brad sold his boat. Within a month, he put his house up for sale. As soon as the deed switched hands, he filled a moving truck and was headed back to New York City where he started. But before those actions, something happened that was far more eventful and important in the scope of things. Susan the yoga instructor called and cried while apologizing into the phone.

Brad valued your call so much that he inspired me to write his story of pre-judging, understanding, and sensitivity. In his words, "Your call meant more to me than anything else in my life. Thank you for your humble and kind words. Again, you have my heartfelt apologies for any pain I caused you. Namaste.".

ABOUT THE AUTHOR

Mitchell Belacone is a native of Manhattan who has been living in Buenos Aires since 2003. The included story "Apples to Empanadas" provides a short biography of the author and his never-ending search for new adventures and experiences. He is the author of *Two Dramas on My Way to Hell* and *Broadway José*.

Made in United States
Orlando, FL
04 June 2023

33798174R00125